Published in The United States of America
By Pogue Publishing, Beeville, TX

Manufactured in The United States of America
First edition published 2017
Cover Design: © 2017, Linda Pogue
Updated Cover: © 2019, Linda Pogue

This cover is based on a design given to the author by
Derek Murphy. Thank you, Derek, for all your help in
learning more about cover design.

**ISBN:** 9781549896095

All characters and events are fiction.

# Wolf's Trust

Lynn Nodima

## Dedication

To my mom and dad. As far back as I can remember,
you both believed I could do anything I set my mind to.
I miss you both so much.

## Please Leave a Review

Please leave a review letting others know what you thought
of this book. Reviews help other readers find books they
will enjoy. They are so much appreciated by readers and
authors!

# Thank you!

## Want to Learn More About Lynn Nodima?

Visit her blog at:

www.lynnnodima.com

# Chapter 1

Daryll carried Zoe out of the office and down the stairs. Dizzy, she swallowed and turned her face against his shoulder to avoid the curious gazes leveled at her when they reached the living room. She felt Daryll's sigh and glanced up to see him shake his head at the *were* people watching them. Only Daryll's arms around her kept her from panic. So many werewolves, and who knew what other kind of *were* animals. He carried her out the front door and settled her back into the front seat of the SUV he drove when he took her to the hospital for treatment for her head injury and snapped her seatbelt.

She watched him walk around the front of the car and slide into the driver's seat. He slammed the door. She jumped and put her hand to her aching head. Daryll looked at her, a frown settled between his eyebrows, but he kept his lips pressed tightly together. He smelled awful. She stared at him, for the first time realizing she splattered his jeans and shoes when she was vomiting. He put the SUV in gear and started driving.

"Where are we going?" The thin sound of her voice surprised her, but then, she never felt so afraid before.

"Nate told me to take you home with me." His eyes cut toward her before returning to the dirt road. "We're going to my house."

Zoe swallowed. The Alpha also told him not to hurt her and not to touch her. That last part confused her. "Where is your house?"

"It's here on the ranch, down the road a bit. We'll be there soon."

A few minutes later, just as the sun slipped down behind the trees, they turned onto another dirt road. Soon it ended in a clearing with five modular homes. In the waning light, Zoe studied the circular drive giving access to a driveway for each

1

house, with an SUV parked at all but one of the houses. All the houses had a large, covered porch built onto the front. The dim light from the porch lights showed each porch had several rocking chairs and swings that looked sturdy enough even for Daryll's lumberjack size and weight.

He pulled the vehicle into the empty driveway and turned off the motor. "This is it."

"Your house?" Zoe frowned when he nodded without looking at her. "You said you have sisters?"

The fear in her voice must have gotten through to him. "Two. They won't hurt you."

"You're sure?"

He finally looked at her, his face holding an odd expression. "I'm sure. They'll know better."

"What? Why?"

Daryll shook his head. He got out and came around the front of the SUV. Opening her door, he leaned in, released her seat belt, and picked her up. Zoe wasn't a large woman, but it impressed her that he lifted her with such ease. He walked up the steps. Before they reached the front door, it opened, and a woman stepped out to hold the door for them. Her nose wrinkled at the smell of them both. Daryll nodded to her, then carried Zoe inside.

Zoe bit her lip, tense, then relaxed slightly against him as she looked around, studying Daryll's home. When he huffed, she looked up at his frown. "Think we lived in caves?"

She felt her face burn and silently cursed the fair skin that would let him see her embarrassment. Unsure what to say, she kept her mouth shut. She glanced again at the living room. The only thing that kept it from looking like any human family lived there was the sturdiness of the furniture. It was built to fit the man holding her.

Warm gold, brown, and rich jades decorated the room, but there were feminine touches, too. Frilled beige curtains draped each window, with matching lace panels defusing the early evening light coming through them. Lace throw pillows made of a coordinating beige fabric were scattered across the furniture. Beige and gold roses filled crystal vases on the tables, while lush green ivy hung in pots suspended from the ceiling in the two back corners.

Zoe glanced at the kitchen. Taupe walls had a backsplash of brown, beige, and turquoise tile, with subtle hints of embedded iron pyrite glinting in the light. Brown tile countertops sported a large, copper double-sink, faucet, and polished copper appliances. Not the colors Zoe would have thought to choose for her own home, but the combination of colors was pleasing, comfortable, homey. She liked it.

Daryll shifted a bit, and she looked up at him. He watched her face as if it really mattered what she thought of his home. He cleared his throat. "Well?"

"You have a lovely home, Daryll." The relief on his face startled her. He grinned, carried her to a recliner covered in brown fabric, and gently set her on it.

The front door closed quietly. Zoe looked at the woman standing beside the door. A frown on her face, the woman looked from Daryll to Zoe, then sighed. She nodded and walked to Zoe. Leaning over, she offered her hand. "I'm Bess, Daryll's oldest sister." When Zoe looked at her hand without responding, Bess sighed again. "You're safe here. No one will hurt you."

Zoe looked up at Bess' sincere brown eyes, swallowed, and shook her hand. "I'm Zoe." She bit her lip, cut her eyes at Daryll, then looked at Bess again. "You're a werebear?"

Light glinted in the woman's eyes. "It's a family thing."

Zoe gave her a strained smile, refusing to cower. "I suppose that makes sense."

Bess laughed and looked at Daryll. "I can see why."

When Zoe turned to follow Bess' gaze, she was surprised to see Daryll's face flush. Ignoring his sister, he dropped on one knee beside the recliner. "Do you think you could eat? Or would you like to clean up first?"

Zoe swallowed and shook her head, then frowned when the movement made the room swing around her. "I'm not sure I could keep anything down. Or stand in the shower."

Bess cleared her throat. "How about some chamomile tea?"

Zoe looked up at Bess. "Tea sounds wonderful."

The front door slammed hard into the living room wall. Zoe jerked and turned to look past Daryll, the sudden movement causing her head to spin and pain to spear through her head. She caught the arms of the recliner in a tight grip. Closing her eyes, she tried to control her surging stomach. Daryll's hand covered her right hand, comforting her.

"Why is she here?"

Zoe forced her eyes open and stared at the belligerent stance of a teen girl, her long brown hair pulled back in a ponytail. Anger burned in the girl's eyes. Zoe swallowed, then sighed in relief when Daryll stood up and stepped between them. Leaning her head to the left, Zoe peered past Daryll at the agitated teen.

"That's enough, Stella."

"But she's..."

Daryll growled. Stella's mouth hung open for a minute, then she shook her head. "Really? You'd growl at me when you bring a Hunter into our house?"

Blinking at the anger she saw in Daryll's stance, Zoe watched him grab Stella by the arm and push her out the open door. He shut the door and the screen quietly behind them. Zoe frowned. She couldn't hear what they said, but the anger in his voice and the belligerence in Stella's came through. Bess walked into the living room from the kitchen and handed her a mug filled with fragrant chamomile tea.

Zoe looked at her. "I'm sorry."

Bess tilted her head and shrugged. "You're a Huntsman. Huntsmen kill *were*. There will be many here who don't want you and your friends to stay, but if the Alpha says you stay, they will eventually accept you." Her eyes twinkled. "That doesn't mean they will like you, but they won't hurt you if you don't try to hurt someone else. Again."

So, Bess knew Zoe stabbed Colonel Marston. Avoiding the older woman's gaze, Zoe looked down at her tea and took a sip. "I won't hurt anyone."

"Good, because the Alpha put you in Daryll's care. If you hurt someone, Daryll will be held responsible."

Zoe swallowed. She glanced up. The intense stare Bess gave her made Zoe twitch. She returned her gaze to the mug in her trembling hands. "I didn't expect Daryll to be so...kind."

Bess laughed. "Because he's a bear?"

"Because..." Zoe looked up and shrugged. "I don't understand. I was taught..." Taking a deep breath, she looked at the woman standing over her. "I was taught *were* want to kill and eat humans. Or change them to *were*."

"You were taught wrong."

"That's what Daryll said."

The front door opened. Stella stomped in and down the hall to her room, slamming her bedroom door behind her. Zoe winced. Daryll followed Stella into the house, a frown on his face. When he looked at Zoe, his frown smoothed away. "Think you could bathe?"

Zoe glanced at the vomit dried on his jeans and shoes, embarrassment again filling her face. "I'm sorry."

He shook his head. "It's okay. You have a concussion." He bowed his head, then peered up at her, uncertainty in his face. "I can help you if you can't wash up alone, or Bess can."

The thought of Daryll being in the bath with her made her shiver. Unsure whether the thought was intriguing or frightening, she pushed it out of her mind. "If Bess can help..."

Bess smiled. "Of course." She studied Zoe for a minute, then nodded. "I think sitting on a stool in the shower would be better than in the tub. Daryll might need to lift you out and..." She bit her bottom lip. Zoe thought she was fighting another smile. "I don't think that would be good for either of you."

Zoe blinked. *Not good for him?* "A shower is fine."

5

With a strict look at Daryll, Bess motioned toward the back of the house. "Off with you, Daryll. You need to clean up even more than she does."

Daryll sighed, nodded, and walked toward the kitchen. He stopped and spun to face Bess. "Nate said to destroy her clothes. He thinks there's a tracker in them."

"It's not in my clothes." Zoe caught her breath and looked down at her hands. She didn't hear him moving, but suddenly, he was bending over her, his hands on the recliner arms.

"Not in the clothes? You know where it is?" His gentle voice was close to her ear, but there was iron in it, too.

Zoe flinched away from him. "It's in my ring."

Daryll picked up her hand and studied the signet she wore. "You're sure?"

"Yes. Only those who worked as interns for the Triumvirate know it's there. It's used as an identifier to help us know other hunters when we see them. Or a locator if we are lost or...run."

"That's how you knew the nurse that tried to kill you was a Hunter?" When she nodded, he asked, "Some of you run?"

She couldn't look at him.

"Zoe, why do some of you run?" When she didn't look up, Daryll curled his fingers beneath her chin and pulled her face up. "Why?"

Zoe blinked, trying without success to force back the tears that pooled in her eyes. "Sometimes, the training is too hard, or someone decides they can't kill, or…"

"Or?"

She shook her head, unwilling to continue.

"What happens to them?"

"Once the oath is taken, a Hunter isn't allowed to ever leave. If they do, they die, or they are taken to the Triumvirate." She swallowed.

"The vampires."

"They're never seen or heard from again." Zoe clenched her eyes closed, trying to still the image of the room whirling around her. "I saw two of the runners die, once. They..." Her fingers caught the wrist of the hand holding her chin. "I can't go back. They'll kill me, too."

Daryll's menacing growl startled her and she looked into his eyes. "No one will take you from me." She shivered at his fierce expression. She bowed her head, staring at the signet ring on her hand.

When he picked up her hand, she glanced at him. "You have to take the ring off, Zoe."

"I can't. It...there's a poison dart in it. If I take it off, I'll die."

The room was so quiet Zoe looked up. Daryll's squatted on his heels, studying her. "You know this how?"

"When runners are brought back, the Triumvirate removes their rings. I saw...they die. Painfully. When their rings aren't taken, they just disappear. They're never seen again."

"But you know what happens to them?"

Zoe swallowed, her breathing quick and shallow at her remembered terror. "I didn't know...I went back for...I lost my phone and needed to find it. I saw...they...I didn't know." She closed her eyes, trying to erase foggy dreamlike images from her mind. "Nate said the Triumvirate are vampires?"

"You saw the vampires attack someone?" Something in Daryll's voice opened her eyes.

Zoe looked at him. Really looked at him. There was shock in his eyes. And sorrow. She nodded and whispered, "She didn't even scream when the...the vampires sucked the blood from her."

"Did the vamps know you saw them?"

"I...don't..." Her gaze darkened, and she thought she would pass out. She shivered, then took a shallow breath. "I don't remember."

Daryll stroked his thumb over the signet ring, frowning. "We'll figure out how to take it off without hurting you, Zoe. For now, wear it. I'll talk to Nate, see if he has any ideas."

Bess put her hand on Daryll's arm. "Enough, for now, Daryll. You get a shower and let me get her cleaned up."

Daryll allowed Bess to pull him away from Zoe, but his gaze stayed on Zoe's face. "You are safe here, Zoe. I won't let them hurt you." Bess waved at him, shooing him away. He spun on his heel and walked through the kitchen to the back of the house, then disappeared down a hall Zoe could barely see from where she sat.

Zoe bit her lip and looked up at Bess' contemplative gaze. "I don't understand."

Bess smiled, sorrow in her eyes. "You will when you feel better." She sighed. "For now, let's get you cleaned up."

# Chapter 2

Peyton Marston, a former Colonel in the Black Forest Huntsman, ran his splayed fingers through his hair. Paige set a cup of coffee in front of him, and he looked up at his daughter. Her smile hid the sadness she didn't want him to see, but her face was too expressive, and he knew her too well to miss it. Sighing, he looked down at his cup.

"I'm sorry, Paige. I'm sorry I ever got us involved with the Huntsmen."

"It wasn't you, Dad. It was Mom."

Peyton swallowed and looked out the RV window. "I wish I..." Peyton bowed his head.

"Mom and Peter weren't your fault, Dad. Mom is the one who insisted that we all be Huntsmen. Mom is the one who talked Peter into going with her. Mom is the one who shot him when he was bitten." Paige sat on the bench across the small table and captured his right hand in both of hers. Her sorrow hit him hard. "Mom killed that wolf's pups, Dad. I won't say she got what she deserved, but she caused it."

The muscle in Peyton's jaw clenched. "Still, I should have tried to get her away from her family when I learned about the Huntsmen."

"You know they wouldn't have let her go. And after you found out about them, they'd have killed you if you didn't join." Paige sighed and squeezed his fingers. "They'll be coming after us, now."

Children's laughter floated on the afternoon breeze, and Peyton looked out the window. Children aged four to fourteen played in the central compound yard. The younger kids played chase, while the older kids played with a softball, throwing to each other in turn across a large circle. Paige, Phillip, and Peter never had the opportunity to be kids. Not really. Thanks to

Pauline. She and her family pulled him into the Huntsmen when he was a young man. It was all his kids ever knew. And that haunted him. Especially now.

The werewolves, werebears, and werepanthers he met since coming to the ranch were nothing like the blood-thirsty, human-hating, human-eating, animals the Triumvirate preached. Peyton shook his head to clear his thoughts and stared at the Huntsman signet ring he still wore. He hated the ring and everything it stood for, now. And he knew removing it would kill him.

A door slammed. Peyton turned to look at the RV parked next to the one he and his two grown kids were living in. A small woman picked up two stacked laundry baskets and started walking toward the main house with an uneven gait. He watched one of the teen boys run up to her. After she briefly fussed at him, she surrendered the laundry baskets to him, and he carried them the rest of the way to the house. Peyton frowned when she followed him, her limp hindering her ability to keep up with the boy.

"That's Nettie."

Peyton pursed his lips and looked at Paige. "What?"

"That's Nettie. Her husband was the Alpha to the Oklahoma Adair Pack until he attacked Janelle. Janelle killed him."

"And Nate brought Nettie here?"

Paige shrugged. "It's a long story, Dad. She was already on her way here when her husband died. He tried to stab Janelle in the middle of the night. Janelle shot him. When Nettie got here, they found out her husband abused her and the kids." Paige refilled Peyton's coffee cup and got herself a cup. "The Oklahoma pack refused to let them come back. Nate gave them a home here."

Leaning back into the upholstered bench back, Peyton sipped his coffee and studied his daughter's face. "He's different than I expected."

"Nate? Yeah. They're all different." Paige sipped her coffee, then set the cup on the table. "Nate wants me and Phillip to join the teens in their training."

"Why? You've both been trained to fight, and you're not wolves."

"He thinks it would help the wolves to know how we were trained." She bit her lip, uncertainty in her eyes before she looked at her coffee cup. "I told him we'd think about it."

"Because of me?"

Paige nodded without looking up.

"Do you want to?"

"I don't know." She swallowed and looked out the window. "I don't want to hurt them, anymore, Dad. I'm not sure I ever did."

When she turned her sorrow-filled gaze back to him, Peyton fought the urge to pull her into his lap like he did when she was a child. "All the things your mother and I taught you were wrong, Paige. It's..." He swallowed hard. "It's hard to say that. Even harder to know it bone deep. These are good people. I can't tell you how much I regret what I've done. What I taught you and your brothers." He took a deep breath and let it out in a rush. "If you want to help them, I won't mind. I won't ask you to if you don't want to, but I won't stop you, either."

He endured her searching gaze. "Nate asked me to help, too. I've already told him I would do anything to help him keep his people safe. Even if it means going against people I believed were my friends. Not because they'll kill me for being here, but because they are wrong."

Her shuddering breath hurt him. He and her mother had done this to her. And Phillip. And Peter, too. Put them in this situation. "I'm sorry I was so wrong, Paige."

"You didn't know. None of us did." Paige stood up and poured the last of her coffee down the small RV sink, rinsed her cup and set it in the drainer. "You want more coffee?"

"No, this is enough."

Paige turned off the coffee maker. "I'm gonna go help

11

Janelle and the other ladies make macaroni and cheese."

Surprise raised his eyebrow. "It takes all of you to open boxes?"

"Homemade. I told Janelle I would shred the cheese for her. She ordered shredded, and it came in huge five-pound slabs." Her hand was on the door latch. "It'll take a while to shred sufficient cheese to make enough for this whole crew, even with a food processor."

Peyton laughed and waved a hand toward the door. "I suppose it will. Go on, then." When she frowned at him, he gave her a smile. "I'm okay, Paige. Just trying to work through some of my baggage."

"If you need..."

"I'll let you know." He met her gaze until she nodded and opened the RV door.

"See you at supper, then." The door closed behind her.

Peyton took the last sip of his coffee. With a sigh, he stood and rinsed his cup, then set it in the drainer. Since his surviving children were never sent on hunts, they didn't have the memories he did, the regrets. Peyton walked to the back of the RV and stretched out on the bed. Nor did they have the nightmares that plagued him since learning he wasn't the protector he thought he was. Instead, he was a murderer.

Four hours later, another nightmare woke him. For a moment, he panicked, not knowing where he was. *We are on the ranch.* Krieges' words vibrated through his mind. Peyton wasn't sure he would ever get used to sharing his thoughts with his wolf. Blinking, he sat up. The sun was still shining, but it wouldn't be for much longer. Swinging his feet to the floor, he wiped his face with both hands. Sooner or later, he needed to accept what he was. A werewolf. A made-wolf, as Nate called him. Eli, Nate's adopted brother, didn't have this much trouble becoming a wolf. But then, Eli hadn't spent the last twenty-eight years as a Huntsman, either.

Peyton walked to the kitchen and pulled a bottle of water

out of the small fridge under the counter. Before he opened it, he glanced out the window. Nettie carried two baskets of folded laundry back toward the RVs, her hip making the distance difficult. Peyton looked for the teens, but they were gone. He set the water bottle on the counter, left the RV, and jogged toward Nettie.

Before he got to her, her eyes widened. Breathing hard, she stopped and took a half-step back toward the main house. Peyton smiled. He reached for the baskets, his hand brushing hers.

With a gasp, she yanked her hands away from his touch. Peyton barely caught the baskets when she jerked away. *She's an abuse victim.* Realizing his approach had frightened her, he stood very still. "I won't hurt you," he said softly.

She swallowed, took another step away from him.

"I'm sorry. I didn't mean to alarm you." He bit his lip. Whatever her husband did, it really messed her up. "I'm going to carry these to your RV, then I'll go away."

He waited until she gave him a slight nod, then turned and hurried to her small home. Setting the baskets on the ground next to the door, he looked at her, head tilted to the left. He turned and took a step toward his RV.

"Thank you."

Without his wolf hearing, he wouldn't have heard her low whisper. He stopped and faced her. "You're welcome. Let me know if you ever need help."

Nettie shook her head. "No. Don't ever do that again." His forehead wrinkled at the fear he felt coming from her. She sidled past him. "Never again." Opening the door, she rushed inside, leaving the clothes baskets where he set them. The door slammed behind her, and the lock clicked.

Peyton sighed and turned away, then spun back when he heard the lock click and the door open. Nettie peeked around the edge of the door at him, her face pale and her eyes wide. Peyton took a step toward her and stopped when she shook her head.

"No." Her voice trembled. "Thank you, but no. I don't want

13

another man. Not again." She stared at him.

"I was just being neighborly when I carried your laundry, Nettie. I won't hurt you."

"That's what he said. In the beginning. But he lied. I think... I think I'm broken. I can't smell lies like most can, so..." She swallowed hard, then whispered, "I just can't take the chance." The door closed quietly. The lock snapped.

# Chapter 3

Daryll was gone when Bess helped Zoe get dressed in sweatpants and a t-shirt after her shower. Feeling better, and definitely smelling better, she allowed the female bear to half-carry her to the bed and set her on it.

Bess helped Zoe lay down, then pulled the sheet over her. "I have some work to do if you don't need me."

"I'm keeping you from work? I'm sorry." A headache throbbed behind Zoe's eyes.

"I can work in here if you want me to. I make jewelry and sell it online so I can set up my work table anywhere. There's enough room to set up in here if you need me."

"If you don't mind, I think I just want to get some sleep." Zoe pressed her fingers to both temples. "My headache is back."

Bess nodded. "If you need anything, just let me know. I'll bring you something to eat in a while. Want the lights out?"

"Yes, please." The light switch clicked, and the room went dark.

After the door closed behind Bess, Zoe relaxed. For a long while, Zoe stared through the dark at the ceiling, trying to relax enough to sleep. She almost fell asleep when she heard footsteps come to the bedroom door. She tensed, afraid Stella was coming to see her. If werebears were anything like werewolves, even a teenager would be powerful enough to kill her.

When the door opened, Bess flipped the light switch and walked in with a tray. Zoe sighed. For some reason she didn't understand, she knew Bess wouldn't hurt her. Bess set the tray on the bed next to Zoe. "I brought you a cream cheese and tomato sandwich on whole wheat and some chicken broth. Try to eat something."

Carefully, ready to just sink back into the covers, Zoe sat up and pulled herself up on the bed to lean against the headboard.

She eyed the sandwich cut into four neat triangles, then picked up the cup of broth and sipped it, not sure she could eat anything solid, yet. Besides, cream cheese and tomato slices? On bread? Somehow, the combination didn't sound good to her.

Bess chuckled, and Zoe looked up at the woman standing over her with her arms crossed over her chest. "Never tried it?" She shrugged. "You might like it. Even without meat on it, Daryll likes it. And he doesn't like many meals that don't include lots of meat on the plate."

Zoe glanced past Bess at the open bedroom door. "Where is Daryll?"

"He's gone for now, but he'll be back." Bess frowned when Zoe twitched, suddenly afraid. "Zoe, nothing will hurt you here. Nothing and no one."

Zoe searched Bess' expression and finally relaxed. Bess believed what she said. Zoe decided to trust her. She sighed and picked up a sandwich triangle and nibbled. Bess grinned at her startled expression at the taste in her mouth, then laughed out loud when Zoe took a large bite and started chewing.

The bear shifter woman sat in the wingback chair by the window. "Good, isn't it?"

Zoe nodded. "It's wonderful." She swallowed and stuffed the last half of the small sandwich triangle into her mouth. After chewing and swallowing again, she stopped and waited to see if her stomach would again rebel. She felt a little nauseated, but then it went away. Suddenly starved, she picked up another triangle sandwich and took another bite.

Zoe managed to eat two of the triangles, half the sandwich, and sip about half a mug of broth when she decided she better not eat anymore. She didn't feel sick, but she did feel too close to it to risk more food. "Thank you."

Bess smiled.

*****

Glancing at Daryll, Nate leaned forward, elbows on the table. "Daryll, unless you oppose it, I want you to take a seat on the Alpha Council to represent the werebears. If you prefer, you can select another, but since we've worked together..." Nate let the sentence hang, his left eyebrow raised in question.

Daryll gave him a solemn nod. "I accept your offer, Alpha. Thank you for including the werebears in your meetings."

Nate gave him a distracted nod. "How is Zoe? Did you destroy her clothes?"

"I think she's better." Daryll frowned. "She said the tracker isn't in their clothes. It's in their rings."

Eyebrow raised, Nate studied his face. "Did you take it?"

"No. According to her, it has a spring-loaded injector with poison that triggers if it's removed. She'll die if I take it off her."

Nate's deep sigh echoed Daryll's. "She sure about that?"

"The vamps take the rings off anyone who runs unless they..." Daryll shook his head and cursed. "Unless they want to eat."

"She knows about the vampires."

Daryll nodded, trying to hide his concern for his mate. "I don't think she was supposed to return from this mission, either."

Nate dry-washed his face with both hands. "I need to search her memories, Daryll."

"I know. You won't hurt her, though?"

"No. If she isn't well enough, I'll wait."

Darcel's satisfied huff didn't surprise Daryll. "I may need someplace else for Stella to stay for a while. She isn't, um, she..." Daryll shook his head, unwilling to say anything that would get his youngest sister in trouble. At the same time, he couldn't allow her to frighten or damage his mate.

"Acts like a teenager? All emotion and drama?"

Relieved, Daryll nodded. "She just doesn't understand, yet."

Nate pursed his lips, then nodded. "Send her to the main house if you need to. We'll keep an eye on her for you."

"Thanks, Alpha."

"Nate." The Alpha raised his eyebrow at Daryll. "My name is Nate."

Daryll couldn't help giving him a grin. "Yeah, I know, but that seems so disrespectful."

With a laugh, Nate shook his head. "I suppose so. I'm just not used to the shifter world, yet. I'll get there."

"You seem to be doing okay."

"Maybe. It's a lot to take in." Nate leaned back in his desk chair. "I'll need someone to be head of security when we convene the council. I'd like you to take that position."

"I don't really have the training for it."

"I know. I'll have Dad work with you. He can provide the expertise, but he doesn't really understand shifters, yet, so I want you in charge."

"Fair enough. I'll do my best."

"That's all I ask." Nate pushed his chair back from the desk and stood up. "Bring Zoe by when she is well enough, I'll talk to her, then."

Daryll nodded. He stood, and Nate walked to the office door with him. "I'll bring her soon."

\*\*\*\*\*

For the next three days, Stella glared at Zoe anytime they were in the same room. So much so that Daryll threatened to send her to stay with the Alpha for a few days if she didn't straighten up. He understood her animosity, but not even his baby sister was allowed to threaten his mate. She would have to learn.

Zoe seemed to feel better. She no longer mentioned headaches or dizziness. Occasionally, she complained she had nothing to do, but the doctor said no television, no reading, nothing that would get her heart rate up. Daryll, much to Zoe's annoyance, followed the doctor's orders to the letter.

Bess stayed with her when she showered or used the bathroom to ensure she had help if she needed it. The rest of the time, Daryll stayed at her side, bringing her water or food. He could tell she was bored but didn't know what he could do about it that wouldn't directly contradict the doctor.

Finally, desperate for something to keep her occupied, he offered to read to her if she would lay still and keep her eyes closed. Daryll wouldn't let her walk anywhere. He carried her to the living room and settled her into his brown recliner, realizing for the first time it was too big for her. *I'll order a new one for her.* He grinned at her sigh and raised his eyebrow. "Well, want me to read or not?"

"How much longer are you going to keep this up?"

Daryll studied her for a moment. "Sure you're not having headaches, anymore?"

"No. I haven't had a headache since yesterday morning."

He grinned at her annoyed scowl, then the grin grew into a smile. "Then you can get up tomorrow. I'll take you to the party."

"What party?"

"Nate is adopting his foster-parents and foster-brother into the *were* family. We've been invited."

The fight went out of her, replaced with fear. "I don't want to go."

"I want you to go."

"Why?"

Her heart started beating faster than it should, and he frowned. "So, you can see we're not the animals you think we are."

She glanced around the living room, then waved her hand to encompass the house interior. "I think you've already shown me that. I...I really don't want to go."

Daryll sighed. "Zoe, I need to take you around the others, so they can see...so they can..." He cleared his throat and blew out a breath. "We'll talk about it next week after you are completely better."

"Talk about what. You keep saying there's something we need to talk about, but you won't talk. Why?"

"I'm afraid you'll be, uh, unhappy about it, and right now, you need to use all your strength to get well."

"Why don't you just tell her?" Stella blew a bubble with her chewing gum.

Daryll looked over his shoulder at Stella. The teen leaned against the front door where she could make a quick escape if Daryll started for her. He frowned. "Stella, go help Nettie get the school ready for classes."

Stella smacked her gum and laughed. "Don't want her to know the 'big bad bear' plans to mate her?"

Daryll surged to his feet, his roar louder than he intended. Seeming to realize she had gone too far, his sister blanched, yanked the door open, and ran. Daryll took a step after her, but Bess was suddenly between him and the door.

"She's just a kid, Daryll. Let me take care of it." Bess put her hand on his arm. He shook her hand off with another growl and gently pushed her aside. Shaking with anger, he took another step toward the door.

"Daryll." Zoe's soft voice pulled him to a stop.

He felt her eyes on his back. He swallowed and struggled to regain his calm, his head bowed. He concentrated on breathing. In, out. In, out. When his breathing was normal, he slowly turned to face her. She was standing in front of his recliner, her hands clenched into fists. "Zoe..." Her name on his lips was a whisper.

"What does she mean, Daryll?" Her gaze trapped his.

He frowned and studied her face, aching at her obvious confusion. "I..." Still searching her face, he took a step toward her. "Darcel, my bear..." He swallowed and shook his head. "Not now. You're not well enough." Turning, he stormed out the front door but stopped long enough to shut it softly, so it wouldn't cause her concussion to give her more pain.

# Chapter 4

Zoe stared at the front door, willing Daryll to come back and explain what she didn't understand. It did no good. He was gone. Sighing, she looked at Bess.

Bess gave her a sad smile. "Can I get you some lemonade or tea?"

"You can tell me what's going on."

Bess glanced at the door, then shook her head. "It's not my place, Zoe. When he's ready, he'll tell you."

"That he wants to mate me?"

Bess sucked her bottom lip into her mouth. "How would you feel about that?"

Zoe blinked. *How would I feel?* She shook her head to clear her thoughts and winced when the pain she thought was gone came back. "How should I feel?"

"Sit down. I'll bring you some tea and we can talk."

"You're going to tell me?"

"Not everything, but I'll try to set your mind at ease."

Zoe nodded and carefully sat back down, then leaned the recliner back. "If you don't mind, I could use some acetaminophen."

"I thought your headache was back. Your eyes are a little glassy looking." Bess walked to the kitchen, removed a pitcher from the refrigerator and filled two glasses with ice and tea. She tucked the bottle of medicine in her pocket, then carried the drinks to the living room. After handing Zoe a glass, she pulled the medicine from her pocket and gave it to her.

Zoe set the glass on the end table, careful to use the tile coaster to prevent damaging the beautiful wood finish. Removing two tablets from the bottle, she swallowed them with a sip of tea, then handed the medicine back to Bess. "Stella said he wants to mate me. I don't understand."

Bess bowed her head, scratched her neck, then peered up at Zoe. "Are you afraid of Daryll?"

"No. He's been nothing but kind."

"Do you, maybe, like him?" Bess watched her face.

Zoe took a sip of tea, paused, then kept her voice noncommittal. "Sure, I like him."

"But do you *like* him?"

"You mean as more than a friend."

Relief showed in Bess' face. She nodded. "Yes."

Zoe thought about the question. She thought about the care he took of her, his gentle touch. She thought about the nurse that tried to kill her and how he stopped her. She thought about him. Tall, at least six-feet, five-inches. Maybe even taller. She thought about his broad shoulders, the strength in his hands and arms, the woodsy, musky scent of him. The dimples in his cheeks when he smiled. Ducking her head to hide the blush she felt climbing her face, she shrugged. "Maybe."

When she finally looked up, Bess was watching her, kindness in her expression. "He likes you. A lot."

"He does?"

"Hmm. How much do you know about *were* and their animals?"

"Not as much as I thought I did. I didn't know there were any *were* but wolves."

Bess laughed and nodded. "Wolves are in literature and history, but the rest of us, well, except for the foxes in Asia, maybe, the rest of us keep a very low profile."

"Why?"

"Because there are those who would hunt and kill us for no reason other than we are shifters."

Again, Zoe felt her face warm. "I can understand that."

"*Were* are two in one body. A human and an animal. In the case of the Crane family, that animal is a bear."

Zoe blinked. "Your family name is Crane?"

With a grin, Bess shrugged. "There's an old story that tells of a cub who brought a single crane home for dinner. Obviously, it wasn't enough for the family to eat, and from that day forward, they called him Crane. Eventually, it became the name for his family."

Taking another sip of her tea, Zoe smiled. "That's cute."

Bess chuckled. "I always thought so. Some of the guys don't appreciate it much, though."

"So, tell me more about being *were*."

"*Were* are able to communicate with their animals." She paused and looked at Zoe for a minute. "Darcel, Daryll's bear, likes you." When Zoe started to speak, Bess held up her hand. "You don't understand. *Were* only have one mate. If they don't find or can't have that one, most won't take a mate. They might date, but never will they settle down and have a family. Ever."

"So, your bear decides who you, uh, mate?"

"Our bear knows, sometimes before we do."

"And it's always right?"

"Always."

Zoe bowed her head. *Daryll wants me for a mate?* She took a deep breath.

After several long seconds, Bess touched her arm. "Breathe, Zoe."

Startled, Zoe realized her head was swimming and gasped a breath. "Sorry. It's just I..."

"It's a bit much to take in, isn't it?"

Zoe nodded. "His bear..."

"Darcel. His bear's name is Darcel. You see, our animals are like another being within us. Almost like two people share one body, except that the body can shift between human and animal."

"Has your bear ever…?"

"No. I haven't found my mate, yet." A mournful look touched Bess' face. "I'm beginning to think I won't find one."

"And if you don't?"

She shrugged. "Then I'll stay with Daryll and make sure he eats right." Bess grinned. "He spends so much time worrying

23

about others he seldom remembers he needs to eat and wear clean clothes."

"It's not just me, is it?"

"No. He was forced to be an Enforcer for an evil Alpha for a long time. He's still trying to make up for what he was forced to do." Bess' eyes filled with tears, and she blinked. "He can't accept that we all know he had no choice. Not if he wanted to keep me and Stella safe. Jackson threatened to kill us if he refused."

Zoe resisted the urge to give Bess a hug. "Jackson. The Arkansas Ozark Alpha?"

"Not anymore. He came here and challenged Nate. Jackson wouldn't quit fighting. Nate warned him, but he just kept coming. Nate killed him in self-defense."

Zoe nearly dropped her tea. She set the glass on the coaster. "Nate? The Alpha here?" She shook her head. "Jackson was so powerful, the Triumvirate sent a full squad after him."

"Nate got him first. The squad found Eli, their new Alpha, and Nate. One of the squad was killed, and Marston was brought here. They sent the rest away."

"Colonel Marston."

Bess gave her a sharp look. "Yes. Colonel Marston."

"Is he alive? Did I...?"

"Did you kill him? Almost." Bess hesitated. "Nate made him a changeling."

"He's a wolf?"

"Yes. He was dying. Nate gave him the choice to live or die. He decided to live."

"He had a choice?"

Bess sighed. "Zoe, I don't know what you've been taught, but changing a human to *were* is difficult and dangerous. It can easily go wrong. Some humans are just not compatible. If they don't die, they become halflings, half animal, half human, neither one nor the other. They usually go insane, becoming a danger to everyone. Maybe in the past, *were* changed humans to *were*. I don't know. But since long before I was born, there's been a general rule that it just isn't done. The Alpha has to approve and supervise to help prevent halflings."

Zoe looked down at her hands. "If I hadn't stabbed him, he would still be human?"

"Yes."

After searching for and seeing the truth in Bess' face, Zoe stood and walked to the window. Holding the curtain aside, she looked out at the children playing in the yard. Werebear children, but they looked human. A movement in the driveway caught her attention, and she watched Daryll. He had the hatchback on the SUV open and sat in the back of the vehicle. Over and over, he slammed his fist into his thigh. His jaw was tight, his eyes bright, and he kept blinking. She frowned at the blood on his hand.

"He's going to bruise himself, and he's bleeding."

Bess stepped up beside her and looked out at Daryll. "He thinks he's lost you before he ever had a chance to tell you he loves you."

Zoe whipped her head to stare at Bess. "He loves me?"

Nodding, Bess sighed. "When your bear decides someone is your mate, you love that person with all your heart. There's nothing he wouldn't do to protect you." She looked at Zoe. "I'm his sister, and he loves me, but if I tried to hurt you, he wouldn't hesitate to destroy me."

Zoe shook her head. "He doesn't even know me. Not really."

"He knows his bear needs you. He knows he needs you. That's all he needs to know. He loves you, Zoe. To him, you're all he ever wanted in a woman. His mate. And he'll guard and protect you for the rest of your life. Even if you don't want him or won't accept him."

Zoe dropped the curtain. Stunned, she walked toward the bedroom. Her hand on the doorknob, she stopped without looking back at Bess. "Tell him to quit hitting himself and...and whatever he's doing that's making him bleed. I can't stand for him to hurt himself like that."

"Zoe, do you…?"

"I don't feel well." Zoe shook her head, not wanting to think about the answer to the question she feared Bess would ask. "I'm going to lay down." She walked into the bedroom, then shut the door behind her.

She leaned back and bumped her head against the door. A sharp pain radiated from her head wound. With a low moan, she pulled away from the door and walked to the bed. Sitting on the edge of the bed, she turned and curled around a pillow that smelled like Daryll. How could she be so wrong about *were* for so long? Why did she still feel the urge to kill? Shoulders shaking, keeping her sobs silent against the pillow, hoping no one heard her, she cried into Daryll's pillow until she fell asleep.

# Chapter 5

When Bess came out and told Daryll what Zoe said about hurting himself, his bear pushed to go to her. Daryll resisted. When he finally went into his bedroom an hour later, she was curled around his pillow, sleeping. He brushed her hair from her face, gently touched her cheek, then he made himself as comfortable as possible on the cot Bess scrounged for him. The next morning, he woke early and hoped Zoe would relax and be more comfortable around him.

She refused to look at him, but she accepted the new summer dress and sandals he ordered for her to wear to the party. She thanked him, but she wouldn't let him touch her. Surprised how much it hurt for her to refuse his help, he left the room while she dressed. When she walked out of the bedroom wearing the sleeveless, turquoise paisley sundress and sandals, he swallowed. She looked so perfect. For the first time since her head wound, Daryll let her walk to his SUV. Most of the werebears walked to the main compound for the party, but he feared she wasn't well enough for that much exertion, yet, and insisted she ride.

Driving toward the main ranch compound, Daryll tried not to glance at Zoe. She was so quiet. Had been since Stella let it slip that Zoe was his mate. She kept her face turned toward the trees on her side of the dirt road Daryll drove over. Finally, he couldn't take the silence anymore.

"Nate wants to meet with you again." His bear snarled at him when her scent changed to pungent fear. "He won't hurt you. He promised me."

For the first time today, she looked straight at him. "Because I'm your mate?"

Daryll's hands clenched the steering wheel. He was going to send Stella to the Alpha's house tonight. Zoe's terror was too much for his bear to handle. He would have to avoid Stella today to prevent mauling her. Swallowing hard, he turned his head just enough to glance at Zoe, then looked back to watch his driving. "I'm sorry that scares you so much. I won't hurt you, Zoe. Ever."

She was quiet for a moment, then sighed. "But I can hurt you, can't I?"

Startled, Daryll slammed his foot on the brake, shoved the gearshift into Park, and turned to look at her. "What?"

"You can't hurt me, but I can hurt you." Her wide brown eyes searched his face. "And you would let me."

Daryll blinked at her, watching her face. "Do you really want to?"

She swallowed, shrugged, and shook her head. "No."

For a moment, Daryll wasn't sure he heard her right. Her scent changed. The fear was gone. In its place was confusion. He started to lick his lips, then stopped, afraid it would frighten her again for the 'big bad bear' his little sister warned her about to lick his lips while looking at her.

She bowed her head and studied her clasped hands. "I keep..." A ragged breath caught in her throat. "I keep having nightmares about..."

When her voice trailed off, Daryll gently tucked a strand of her blond hair behind her ear. Barely able to speak, he whispered, "Zoe?"

"I keep seeing the Triumvirate killing my friends. I keep hearing them tell me to...kill the *were*."

Daryll put his curled fingers beneath her chin and turned her face to his, then cupped her face in his palm. "Tell me."

At his soft insistence, she shuddered. "I don't really remember. It's like they're whispering in my mind." Her hand caught the wrist of the hand he held against her face. "I hear them commanding me to, but I..." She took a deep breath. "I'm so afraid I'm going to hurt you. Kill you."

Daryll tilted his head, trying to catch her gaze. "Do you want to?"

"No...yes...I don't know. I don't want to, but I keep feeling like I have to." She raised her gaze to his and whispered, "Don't let me hurt you, Daryll. I don't want to hurt you."

He nodded. "I won't let you hurt me if you really don't want to."

She took a shuddering breath and pulled away from his hand. Sniffing, she looked out the windshield, staring with glazed eyes at the dirt road. "Don't let me hurt anyone."

"Nate can stop them. Keep them from forcing you to do anything you don't want to do."

Uncertain eyes looked back at him. "He can?"

"He can." Realizing she wasn't afraid of him, but instead that she might hurt him, he smiled. "Until then, I'll be careful and watch over you. You won't hurt anyone. I promise."

She blinked and wiped her right eye with the heel of her right hand. "Thank you," she said, her voice soft. "I don't understand. I never really wanted to hurt anyone, before, and I... tried to kill Paige's dad. I saw it happen. I knew it was me, but it was like I was out of control. Like I was watching a movie I couldn't stop."

"You think the vamps were controlling you?"

"I don't know. I just don't know."

Daryll sighed. "The ceremony will start soon, but I'm taking you to Nate. Maybe he can..." He gave her a sad smile. "I think he can take away whatever subconscious commands the vamps gave you." When she nodded, he started back toward the compound, hoping Nate would have time to see her before the party.

*****

Nate looked up when Daryll tapped on the office door. He frowned when he saw Zoe hiding behind the big werebear's back. The smell of her fear reached him, and he looked at Daryll.

Daryll clenched his fists and gave Nate a tight nod. "We need to talk with you, Nate."

29

"Come in. Shut the door."

Daryll reached behind him and gently pulled Zoe into the room, then shut the door. She was trembling so much she was unsteady on her feet. Daryll sighed and picked her up, then walked to the chairs across the desk from Nate. Sitting, he settled her into his lap. Nate watched the girl shiver and turn her face toward Daryll's chest.

"I think the vamps have her under compulsion to kill." Nate raised an eyebrow but stayed quiet when Daryll spoke again. "She asked me not to let her hurt me or anyone else. Please help her."

Frowning at Daryll's concern, Nate leaned forward, elbows on the desk, hands steepled. "Zoe, the only way I can help you is to have Koreth go through your memories."

Without looking up, she nodded.

Nate walked around the desk and sat on the edge, looking down at the girl in the bear's arms. "Look at me, Zoe."

When she raised her eyes to his, he saw terror. Terror that morphed into killing hatred. She surged from Daryll's arms, her hands moving to Nate's throat. As her hands closed around his neck, Nate caught her wrists and held her hands away from him, watching her eyes. Daryll caught her by the waist and pulled her back into his lap away from Nate. She twisted against his hold, then her eyes cleared. Zoe blinked several times, then her eyes filled with tears and she slumped. Nate allowed her to fall back against Daryll's chest and watched her body spasm into deep, painful shudders.

He shifted. Koreth told Darcel to have Daryll hold her so that he could see her face. Startled, she looked into the Alpha wolf's glowing eyes. Koreth gently pushed into her mind, careful to slide past the parts of her mind that were still pained from her injury, past her most recent attempt to kill him, past her visit to the hospital and the nurse's effort to kill her, back to the last time she stood before the Triumvirate, then back further.

Zoe and another Huntsman marched to the Triumvirate office, both clasping an arm of the two captured runaways. The runaways, both young, a man and a woman barely past their teens, stumbled down the hall but did not try to escape. When the door opened to let them into the Judgement Hall, Zoe's compatriot pulled the young man before the three officers. Summarily judged unworthy, one of the Triumvirate snatched the man's hand and removed the ring from his finger. The Huntsman screamed. A tiny bead of blood popped out on his ring finger where the ring had been, then he dropped to the floor, writhing in pain for long minutes before he stopped breathing.

The woman Zoe held sobbed once, then was silent. Zoe's partner bent and caught the dead man's arms and dragged him out the door. Trembling at what she had witnessed, Zoe stepped up, pulling the woman to the three. The three looked at her prisoner for several seconds, then the man in the center smiled, mirthless, deadly.

"Leave her here," he commanded. Zoe saluted and turned toward the door. She was almost to her quarters when she realized her phone was missing. She knew she had it when they met the van bringing in the two runaways. Returning to the truck bay, she walked the path but didn't find it before she got back to the Judgement Hall. Listening at the door, she didn't hear anything. Carefully, ready to slip back out if she was disturbing the Triumvirate, Zoe stepped into the room and stopped. Her mouth dropped open in a silent scream.

The three members of the Triumvirate surrounded the young woman Zoe delivered to them. Two held her wrists to their lips, the third stood behind her, his mouth open on her neck. The judge holding the woman's left wrist looked up and saw Zoe standing at the door. Zoe turned to leave, but before she could get the door open again, moving inhumanly fast, he had his hand wrapped around the back of her neck. He pulled her to the others.

Zoe's fear threatened to stop her heart when the vampire lowered his mouth to her neck. Koreth pushed her into the role of observer rather than participant, shielding her conscious mind from the fear evoked by the memories. Still, he continued to go forward until he felt the blood geas the vampires laid on her. A command to go with Paige to find Phillip, then kill her, her brother, and her father, if they still lived. They ordered her to attack the *were* Alpha afterward and kill as many *were* as she could. Koreth frowned, captured the geas, surrounded it with his power, and dissolved it, freeing Zoe from her need to kill.

Gently, more careful leaving than when entering, Koreth crept out of Zoe's mind. As soon as his mind was free of hers, he shimmered into Nate. Nate looked down at the unconscious girl's face, then looked at Daryll. "She was programmed to kill the Marston's, then me, then the rest of the *were*. Koreth removed the command to kill."

Daryll looked down at her. "Is she...?"

"She'll be okay. She should be herself soon, but she's still healing. Give her time."

Daryll nodded. "Thank you, Alpha."

"I told you..."

"Yes, Sir, but only an Alpha more powerful than I could have saved her. Thank you."

Nate studied the relief in Daryll's eyes. He thought of his mate, Janelle, of how it would hurt if she wanted to kill him. Taking a deep breath, he nodded. "You're welcome."

# Chapter 6

Following a short, emotional adoption ceremony where a werewolf named Dusty Mercer, and Nate's foster family, Major Curtis Thomas, his wife Cynthia, and his son Eli, were adopted into the pack as the family of the Alpha, the *were* gathered at the picnic shelter. Community-sized barbecue pits provided enough barbecue beef, sausage, and chicken to feed the gathering, while two tables were filled with huge trays and bowls of pickle spears, sliced onions, potato salad, coleslaw, pinto beans, cornbread, and dozens of sliced watermelons. Off to one side of the shelter, teen boys took turns cranking the handles on nearly two-dozen old-fashioned ice cream freezers. Teen girls teased the boys. Warehouse-sized fans at the periphery of the picnic shelter helped make the mid-August Texas heat bearable.

Zoe stood off to the side, leaning against one of the poles supporting the shelter roof, watching and hoping no one would identify her as the woman who attacked Colonel Marston last week. So far, most people ignored her. When Daryll growled at the few that didn't, they walked away. The shifter stood next to her, almost as if he was protecting her against the multitude of werebears, werepanthers, and werewolves at the party.

It seemed the fact that she was allowed to be here was reason enough to leave her alone. Well, that and the huge man standing behind her seeming to dare anyone to challenge him. Zoe was starting to tire. After nibbling the barbecue Bess brought her, she finally gave up all pretense of being hungry and looked at Daryll. "How soon can I leave?"

Daryll looked down at her and frowned. "What's wrong? Are you okay?"

"Just tired, I think." Zoe glanced around the shelter, her gaze drawn to the Alpha being scolded by his mate. He looked abashed as if caught doing something he shouldn't. As soon as

Janelle turned her back, he dipped his little finger in barbecue sauce and offered it to baby Ophelia. The look on Janelle's face when she turned and caught him again offering barbecue sauce to the infant brought the ghost of a smile to Zoe's lips.

The two looked for all the world like human parents squabbling over how to feed a baby. While Janelle fussed at Nate, one of the boys, Zoe thought he might be nine or ten years old, slipped past Nate and handed Ophelia a small stuffed kitten. The infant gurgled a laugh and clutched the small toy in both hands.

"Zoe?"

Zoe caught her breath and turned to face Paige. Paige's hesitant smile speared through Zoe. Turning away from Paige, Zoe took a step, running into Daryll's brawny chest. His hands caught her shoulders to keep her from losing her balance. He looked down at her, and she shook her head. "I can't," she whispered. "I just can't."

Sadness and sorrow entered his eyes. Before she could object, he caught her up in his arms and strode toward the SUV he drove to the party. Zoe peeked over his shoulder to see Paige watching him carry her away. Paige had her bottom lip between her teeth as if she still cared about Zoe. *How could she care? I tried to kill her father, and now he's one of the wolves!*

She ducked her face into Daryll's chest and struggled not to cry. Paige, her only friend the entire time she grew up. The only one who ever understood how hard being a Huntsman really was. *How can Paige possibly forgive me for what I've done?*

Daryll settled her into the front passenger seat of the interior, buckled her belt then dashed around the front of the SUV to get into the driver's seat. The air conditioner blasting, trying to rid the vehicle of summer heat. Daryll put the car in gear. As it started to roll forward, he slammed his foot on the brakes. Zoe looked up to see Paige standing in front of the SUV, arms crossed. Paige tilted her head and sighed, then motioned to the side. When Zoe's door opened, Daryll growled. Zoe flinched away from Paige's brother, Phillip.

34

Phillip ignored the angry bear behind her and leaned down to face her. "We need to talk, Zoe."

When she didn't hear anger in his voice, Zoe raised her gaze to meet Phillip's. "I don't..."

"We have to talk." He pressed his lips together, then sighed. "Nate told us the Triumvirate forced you to do what you did. Please. Just come talk to us. We need your help."

*They need my help?* "I don't understand," she finally said.

"The Huntsmen turned on us. All of us. We've learned how wrong they are, and we want to stop them. Will you help us?"

Zoe pondered Phillip's soft words. She studied his eyes, realizing he believed he could do something. "They'll kill you. They already want you dead."

"So, help us stop them." Phillip glanced toward the center of the compound where a large group of children chased each other, shrieking and laughing in their play. "Let's keep them from destroying the children here."

Zoe followed his gaze to the kids playing chase. She ignored Daryll's hand on her shoulder. Looking back at the shelter, she watched the teen boys cutting up and laughing while they cranked the ice cream freezers and the girls flirting with them. She looked past the teenagers and watched Nate pull Janelle in his arms and kiss her, trying, Zoe thought, to get out of trouble for feeding the baby barbecue sauce. She glanced at Ophelia. Ophelia, the first baby wolf she'd ever seen, looked human. A sweet, tiny, innocent infant girl with the cutest blue eyes.

She swallowed, then looked back at Phillip. "I tried to kill your dad."

"You were conditioned and forced to try to kill him. And me. And Paige." Phillip grinned. "You want to go after the vampires with us for controlling you? For trying to kill us all?"

Zoe frowned at Phillip. "You trust me?"

"Nate said he removed the geas forcing you to try to kill us. I trust him." He tilted his head. "I trust you, Zoe. So, does Paige."

Zoe turned to look out the windshield at Paige. Her best

35

friend smiled at her. She studied Paige's face, looking for deceit or anger. What anger she saw wasn't directed at her, but at the Triumvirate. Zoe bit her lip. Pulling away from Daryll's tight grip on her shoulder, she looked at Phillip. "What is it you want me to do?"

"The four of us know the Huntsman HQ layout. We know who might help and who will definitely be against us. And we know where the safe houses are." He nodded. "Our knowledge is a secret weapon to help the pack stop the Triumvirate." Phillip extended his open right hand toward her. "Help us stop the killing."

Zoe bowed her head. For the first time in too long, she felt like herself. Strong, well-trained, capable. She thought about the fear Koreth had shielded her from. Thought about the feel of a vampire's teeth on her neck, using compulsion to force her to feed him and follow his instructions. She raised her left hand to her throat, pressing against the hidden bite mark she could still feel.

Behind her, Daryll sniffed, then leaned forward and sniffed her neck. A deep growl vibrated against her back and she felt his warm face press against her neck, his raspy tongue licking away the memory of the vampire's teeth. She felt Daryll's teeth graze her neck and shivered, then turned to face him. His eyes glowed like amber gold. "I will remove his touch. You will never feel it again."

Startled, she watched him dip his face into her neck and closed her eyes, feeling the warmth, and comfort of his mouth on her. She swallowed. He moved away, his gaze fixed on hers. "I will protect you always, Zoe. They'll never touch you again."

She didn't understand the way his words filtered through her, releasing her fear. Surprised her trembling stopped, she reached up and touched his face. "Because I'm your mate?"

Behind her, she heard the sharp intake of Phillip's gasp, but it wasn't important. She kept her eyes on Daryll's face. For the barest moment, she saw fear in his eyes, then he blinked and

36

slowly nodded. "Because you're my mate," he whispered. "Whether you ever accept me or not, Zoe, I'll protect you forever."

Zoe sat very still, looking into Daryll's expressive eyes. Without turning to look at Phillip, she nodded. "I'll help you, Phillip, but not now. Right now, I need to go home."

Daryll's right eyebrow twitched. "Home?"

She nodded. "Your home, Daryll. Take me home and explain this to me."

Daryll swallowed. "Shut the door, Phillip. We'll be back to talk with you later."

"Zoe?" Phillip's voice was strained. "Mate?"

Zoe's gaze never left Daryll. "Shut the door, Phillip." She heard the door shut softly behind her. Daryll blinked and moved back into the driver's seat. He waved Paige to the side, waited until she moved, then drove toward the werebear compound. Home.

# Chapter 7

When Zoe stepped out of the SUV, she stumbled. Without a word, Daryll caught her before she hit the ground, then set her back on her feet. She tilted her head back to look up at him. Compared to her petite five-feet, two-inch height, he was a giant. For a brief second, she hesitated at the intensity of his gaze, then took a deep breath and walked past him to the stairs. She swayed dizzily on her way up the stairs, and felt his hand on her waist, steadying her. Somehow, he knew she didn't want him to carry her into the house. Wanted to go on her own two feet so that he would know she wanted to be there.

He reached past her to open the door and hold it for her. Zoe stepped into the house, then walked to the loveseat. She wouldn't sit in his recliner. Sitting, she looked up at him. The emotions moving across his face were confusing. She saw longing, compassion, and...Zoe frowned. Commitment showed in his eyes, tainted by fear. She shook her head, wondering how the werebear could fear anything, then remembered what Bess told her. *He thinks he's lost you before he ever had a chance to tell you he loves you.*

Her voice soft, Zoe smoothed the frown from her face. "Bess said you love me."

"And that scares you?"

Zoe forced herself to face his scrutiny, forced herself not to hide her face from him. "A bit." She raised her shoulders in a slight shrug. "You're *were*. I've been taught all my life that you will eat me."

A smile tugged at his lips, barely turning up the corners, but it lit his eyes. "And now?"

Zoe struggled not to grin at him. "Now, I don't know what to believe."

"I will never hurt you, Zoe. I won't let anyone else hurt you, either."

Absolute certainty filled his tone, wrapped Zoe in comfort she couldn't remember ever feeling. "Even if I try to hurt you?"

"If you do, it will be because you want to, not because the Triumvirate forced you. Nate removed the geas they had on you."

"You're sure?"

"That's what he said. He's the Alpha. He can't lie to pack."

"So, you're safe? From me?" Zoe searched his face, looking for any uncertainty, any hint of an untruth. "I won't wake up one night and try to kill you all?"

"Is that what you're afraid of?"

When Zoe nodded, he dropped to one knee in front of her. With his height, even on one knee, he was still slightly taller than her when she was sitting. He put his hands on her shoulders and gave her a light squeeze. "Zoe, I trust you not to hurt me or my family. I've listened to you talk in your sleep, begging the vampires not to force you to hurt us. Now that Nate has dissolved the geas, I know you won't do anything to us. I just know it."

Zoe swallowed. She pressed a tentative palm against his face. "I wish I was as certain as you are." She leaned forward and touched her lips to his forehead, then leaned back when he moved to take her into his arms. "Until I am certain, until I know I won't hurt you...until then..." Zoe gave him a trembling smile. "Until then, I can't be what you want me to be."

"And when you are certain?" Waves of pain came from him.

Zoe held her breath and wondered how she could feel his pain. "Until then, I'll stay here, but I can't..." She shook her head, unwilling to say the words he needed to hear.

Daryll pressed a finger to her lips. "Until then, I won't be your mate, but you will always be mine."

*****

39

*Mine!* Daryll struggled to control the angry bear inside him. All he needed was to change and scare her to death. *Not now. Give her time!* He closed his eyes, trying to make Darcel understand that she hadn't said never, just not yet. Darcel roared in his mind. Shaking with the effort to control his bear, Daryll stood up and took a step away from her.

"I have to go out for a while." He hated the fear that jumped into her eyes when his voice turned so guttural. "I'll be back."

"Daryll?"

Ignoring the pleading in her voice, he rushed outside, shut the door as quietly as he could manage with his bear raging at him, and ran toward the cave beyond the old line cabin beyond the trees. Before he was out of sight of the house, Darcel burst out of him. Not the gentle shimmer shift Daryll was used to, but a violent, wrenching surge into a bear. Darcel forced him to stop his headlong race for the cave on the other side of the creek behind the trees and turned back toward the house.

Zoe stood on the porch, watching him. The smell of her fear coiled around Darcel. He stood on his hind legs, and threw his head back, roaring his pain at his loss. When he focused on her again, he blinked, startled. Zoe walked across the lawn toward him. There was fear in her eyes, fear he could smell stronger as she approached. She stopped about ten feet from him. Darcel whimpered and dropped to all fours to try to lessen her fear. He sat and looked at her. *Mine is afraid of me!*

Zoe swallowed. Darcel sat very still, trying not to frighten her more. Slowly, Zoe moved closer with uncertain steps, then closer. When she reached an unsteady hand toward Darcel, he whimpered again but held still. She gently set her hand on his head between his ears. *Don't move, Darcel. Don't scare her!* Darcel twitched his ears, annoyed his human didn't trust him.

Hand still on his head, she stepped closer, then ruffled her fingers through the fur between his ears. Almost as if afraid he would snap at her fingers, she trailed her hand down the side of his face. Her gaze met his eyes, and Darcel blinked. He tilted his head to the left and, careful to keep his teeth away from her hand, licked her fingers. For a moment, she froze. Darcel whined and leaned away from her.

"You really won't hurt me." The wonder in her tone brought Darcel's gaze to her face.

The rancid smell of fear disappeared. In its place, a sweet, honeysuckle fragrance tickled his nose. This was the smell of his mate when she was calm. Darcel raised his paw, stroked her cheek with the back of his paw, keeping his claws away from her. When she didn't flinch, Darcel leaned forward. She didn't move away; he dropped his paw, leaned forward, and licked her face from chin to forehead. She tensed for a moment, then laughed. When she laughed, he roared his approval and released his hold on Daryll.

Darcel shimmered into Daryll. Zoe wiped the bear's saliva off her face. "Eewww!"

Daryll laughed at the face she made. "Darcel likes you."

"You think?"

Daryll stopped laughing. He wasn't sure how to take her sarcastic tone.

"At least I know I'm not on the supper menu." Zoe rolled her eyes, then grinned at him. "I've never been that close to a bear before."

Lips pursed, Daryll shook his head. "None of the other bears will dare to come that close to you, Zoe. They know better."

"Werebears, or all bears."

"All *were* and all animals. None will bother you. Ever. You are safe with me." He frowned. "At least you will be when we are mated."

"Because grizzlies are the top of the food chain?"

"Something like that."

"And if we're not mated?"

"I'll protect you with my life, Zoe, but I can't guarantee another *were* won't try to take you as a mate." In his mind, Darcel roared. *Mine! None will take her!* Daryll tried to keep Darcel's thoughts off his face.

"But if we mate, no one else will, um, try?"

"No. Not unless they have a death wish. If so, I'll be happy to grant that wish."

"You would kill for me?"

"I will protect you. Whatever it takes. Even if you don't mate me, but it will not be as easy if we are not mates."

She sighed. "I don't understand."

"Zoe, if you are not a claimed mate, any shifter can challenge for you. I would fight to keep you from them if you didn't want to go with them, but if it's another bear or Alpha, I might not be able to stop them."

"But if I was claimed?"

"None would dare. The Royal Alpha, Nate, would back me if any tried, and it would be certain death for them. They would have to kill Nate as well as me, which wouldn't be as easy as you might think."

"So, Nate would protect us both if we mated?"

Daryll nodded. "As Alpha, it's his responsibility to keep peace in the pack and to protect us. If any tried to take you, he would stop them, even if I couldn't."

"Can we sit on the porch? It's awfully hot out here in the sun."

Watching close to make sure she wasn't uncomfortable with his action, Daryll took her hand and walked toward the house. Aware that she was trembling with fatigue, he walked at her pace. He helped her to one of the porch rockers, then pulled another rocker close to her and sat facing her. "Are you alright?"

"I'm okay."

Daryll frowned at the shivers the lie sparked across his shoulders. *Our mate is brave!* Daryll shook his head at his bear and focused on Zoe. "Do you need anything?"

"No. Yes. I need some water."

"Wait here." Daryll went inside and filled a glass with ice

water. When he returned, she was gazing across the Texas timberland. "Here you go."

Zoe accepted the glass and took several small sips, before nodding and setting the drink on the edge of a table holding a large pothos ivy. "Thank you." Without looking up, she cleared her throat. "May I ask you something?"

"You can ask me anything."

"Anything?" Her startled eyes darted up to look at Daryll.

"Anything."

She looked at her hands folded in her lap. After a moment, she cleared her throat. "I never knew there were werebears or other shifters except for werewolves." She swallowed but kept her eyes down. "Are werebears, are they, I mean, do werebears...?"

"Do werebears what?"

"Do you, um, have to change on the full moon like, um, werewolves do?"

Daryll's laughter brought her gaze up. "No, and werewolves don't have to do that, either."

"They don't?"

"No. It's a myth."

"But the Huntsmen said the full moon was the best time to..." Her face reddened, and she ducked her head again. "To hunt."

"It probably is." Daryll's quiet words brought her gaze to his face. "The moon's pull is stronger on the full moon, but it doesn't force any of us to shift. Traditionally, the full moon is the time of gatherings for mating rituals. It's an old tradition, not followed as much, anymore. During the mating ritual, the *were* shift to their animals. That's probably where the myth came from."

"So, the moon doesn't...?"

"Control us? No." He tilted his head, trying to see her downturned face. "What?"

"Tell them not to mate on the full moon, anymore. That's

43

when the Huntsmen are most likely to attack." Her soft words made the hair on the back of his neck stand up.

"Will they attack this full moon?" When she didn't answer, Daryll leaned forward and caught her hands in his. "Zoe, tell me. That's only two days from now."

Zoe shrugged, shame on her face. "I don't know, Daryll." The chirps of crickets and katydids filled the silence between them. When she looked up, Daryll caught his breath. The pain radiating from her eyes wasn't physical. "I need to talk to Colonel Marston if he...if he'll talk to me."

"Only if I stay with you." Daryll thought she would argue, but after studying his face for a moment, she nodded.

"You can stay."

Daryll scooped her up from the rocker and carried her back to the SUV. Her arm across his shoulder, she watched his face. When he set her on the seat, he raised an eyebrow at her. "What?"

"Are you going to carry me from now on?" She blushed. "I can walk, you know."

"You haven't been cleared by a doctor."

"I won't regain my strength if you don't let me exercise."

"I know."

"But?"

Heat rose up his neck and he knew his face was red. "When you're well, you won't need me."

Zoe laughed. Daryll tilted his head and searched her twinkling eyes. "I don't have to be sick or hurt to need you, Daryll." Her mouth dropped open, then she caught her bottom lip in her teeth and blinked as if she hadn't intended to say that out loud.

Daryll grinned at her, suddenly happy. "Good to know. Let's go see the Colonel." His step felt much lighter on his way around the car to the driver seat. He slid behind the steering wheel and buckled his seatbelt. "I think we should have Nate there."

"Not this time. I need to... We need to talk, first, so we can

44

decide how we can best help the pack."

Unable to prevent tensing at her words, Daryll glanced at her. "What are you talking about?"

"I think between us, Paige, Phillip, the Colonel, and I may know enough about the Huntsmen to help you stop their plans, but we all have to be willing to do this for it to work. If Nate is there, I think it will make it harder to agree to help. Phillip said they want to help the *were*, but I have family still with the Huntsmen. I need to talk with the Marston's."

"With me there." He wasn't asking. If she was meeting behind Nate's back, he would be there to make sure the pack's interests were covered. Whether she wanted him there or not.

Zoe nodded and looked at him. "You can smell a lie, right?"

"Um, yeah."

"So, if you want to know anything, just ask. You'll know if any of us lie."

"As long as you understand, Zoe, you are my mate, and in almost anything, you come first, but until the mating is accomplished, my pack's safety comes first." He glanced at her, then turned back to driving. "I won't go through with the mating if there is any chance it will be used against the pack."

When she didn't answer, he glanced at her again. She nodded. "I will never put you in that position, Daryll. I promise."

The truth in her words settled between his shoulder blades, left comfort and relief in their wake. "Thank you," he whispered, relieved battling Darcel for control wasn't necessary. If she'd lied to him... Darcel was almost all instinct, and she was his mate. Daryll was intelligence as well as instinct. He would follow the right path for his pack, but if it was against Zoe, he would suffer for it. More than Zoe would ever know. Darcel would destroy him.

# Chapter 8

Early evening Texas sunlight filtered through the trees, as the sun dropped over the hills to the west. The temperature cooled slightly. Daryll glanced at the skies. *Clear night tonight, it'll be even cooler later.* There was still a crowd at the picnic shelter. Some of the teens were lighting lanterns that hung in the shelter rafters, but Daryll took a chance that Colonel Marston, Paige, and Phillip returned to the RV assigned to them. When he pulled up beside the RV, the interior lights were on, and the curtains pulled back. He could see them sitting at the small table inside.

When he turned off the engine, Paige glanced outside, said something to her family, then moved to the door. Daryll walked around the SUV, opened Zoe's door, then grinned at her. "I can carry you, or you can walk." His grin widened when her cheeks bloomed with pink.

"I'll walk."

Daryll nodded and stepped back to let her out of the SUV. Staying close behind her, he followed. As she reached the door, Paige opened it. The two young women stared at each other for a minute, then Paige came down the steps and hugged Zoe. "I'm so glad you're okay, Zoe!"

Zoe pulled back and looked at her. "What?"

"When Daryll took you to the hospital, I wasn't sure you'd be coming back. You had blood all in your hair and you were…"

"Vomiting." Zoe grinned and cast a quick glance at Daryll. "All over Daryll."

The werebear harrumphed and shrugged. "You were hurt."

"Paige, I'm…"

"The Alpha told us the vampires put a compulsion on you to force you to kill Dad." Paige gave her another hug. "We know you wouldn't do that if you were in your right mind."

"You know they're vampires?"

From behind Paige, Colonel Marston cleared his throat. "Nate told us." When Daryll looked at him, the Colonel nodded to him, then motioned them inside. "Come on in. If you're here to help, we'll take all we can get."

Zoe let Paige pull her into the RV, and Daryll followed. He shut the door behind him, conscious of the air conditioner humming in an effort to keep the Texas heat out of the small RV. It might be cooler than it was earlier, but it was still warm outside.

Zoe motioned toward Daryll. "Have you met Daryll Crane?"

"I've seen him around, but we haven't met." Colonel Marston put his hand out, and Daryll shook it. "Welcome to our home, such as it is."

Daryll glanced around and nodded. "Thank you. I'm sure you'll have a better home when all this is over. The Alpha takes care of his pack."

Colonel Marston looked a bit surprised, then cleared his throat. "Well, it's enough for now. Let's have a seat."

"Thank you, Colonel."

"Peyton. Call me Peyton. I'm not a Colonel in the Huntsmen, now."

Daryll grinned and nodded. "Call me Daryll."

"Have a seat." Peyton slid onto the u-shaped booth bench. Paige slid in beside him. Phillip slid in opposite Paige and around to the back. Zoe sat and moved to give Daryll room to sit.

After everyone was in place, Peyton shrugged. "We never knew the Triumvirate were vampires. Nate searched all our memories and found evidence of compulsion geas. He removed those." He glanced at Paige and Phillip. "We've decided to join the pack in their efforts against the Triumvirate, but at the same time, we're hoping to minimize human casualties. Nate wants us to hunt the Huntsmen and try to get them to join us."

Daryll nodded. So far, everything Peyton said was true. "And you want Zoe to help?"

Peyton glanced at Zoe and nodded. "Zoe and I have the

most top-level information. She may know some things I don't, so it would really be helpful for her to be a part of this."

Zoe opened her mouth, but before she could speak, Daryll's hand closed over the hand she rested on the tabletop. "I won't allow you to endanger her."

Peyton blinked, then his eyes grew wide. "Does she know?"

"She does."

"Did she agree?"

Daryll ignored the questions in Paige's and Phillip's faces. "Even if she never agrees, I will not allow it."

Peyton leaned back, staring at Daryll. Mouth closed, then he sucked air between his front teeth. For a moment, he reminded Daryll of Nate, then the thought was gone. Peyton leaned toward Daryll. "As the closest thing to family Zoe has here, I will not allow mating unless it is what she wants."

Darcel started growling deep in Daryll's chest, but before he could respond, Zoe laid her free hand on top of the hand Daryll held over her left hand. "That's enough, both of you." She tilted her head at Marston. "He's already promised he will give me the choice and won't pressure me. And Nate told Daryll he won't allow it if I don't want it."

Peyton's eyebrow twitched. "Nate knows?"

"He does." Daryll tried to keep the growl out of his voice and winced when he didn't quite make it. "I won't take advantage. It's her choice. Even so, if she goes into danger, I go with her."

"Um, what's going on?" Paige looked from her dad to Zoe to Daryll and back to her dad. "Dad? Zoe?"

"Darcel, Daryll's bear, wants to claim me." Zoe's tone was neutral. Daryll glanced at her, but nothing in her expression told him what she thought of the idea. She shrugged and sighed. "I don't know what I want, yet, but I'm willing to think about it."

"Oh, Zoe!" Paige bit her lip. "Does that mean you'll be a werewo...um, werebear?"

Zoe blinked and looked at Daryll. "I don't know. We haven't really talked all it means."

Daryll rolled his eyes. "That's not what we came here for." Bear though he was, he felt outnumbered and uncomfortable with the three Marston's looking at him. Daryll scratched his neck with his free hand.

"As long as it's her choice and Nate is aware, I'll stay out of it." Peyton took a deep breath and frowned. "But if she says no..."

"If she says no, it's no. I know that." Daryll met Peyton's stern gaze until the other man finally grinned.

"I can hear the truth, too, now, you know."

"Yeah. Wolves are a pain in the..." Daryll stopped muttering and grinned back at Peyton. "Most shifters can do that. What's this about stopping the Huntsmen?"

Peyton smirked. "That's not quite what you intended to say, but we'll let that go."

"Colonel..."

"Peyton, Zoe. I'm not a colonel, anymore."

Zoe waved a hand. "Peyton, did you know the full moon thing is a myth?"

Peyton looked startled and glanced at Daryll. "A myth?"

"A myth. I don't know when it started, but it isn't true. Wolves and some of the other shifters traditionally gathered on the full moon for mating rituals. That's why they were often wolves then, not because they were under the moon's power or anything like that." Daryll lifted both shoulders and dropped them. "Some packs still do, but not all. This pack doesn't."

"Interesting." Peyton looked at Zoe. "Is there some significance?"

"I don't know which full moon, but the Triumvirate is planning to attack on a full moon."

Marston glanced at Paige and Phillip. "We were afraid there might be an attack soon, but it didn't occur to me it would have anything to do with the phase of the moon."

Daryll sighed. "I don't really understand the significance, myself."

"If the Huntsmen kill *were* with silver bullets while they are wolves…" When Zoe's words stopped, she looked into his eyes. "Do you understand now?"

Daryll closed his eyes, bowed his head, and huffed. "When *were* die from silver poisoning while under shift, they don't shift back to human after death. There can be no murder charge against them. There's no proof they killed people." If *were* died any other way, they returned to human after death, but if they died with silver in their veins, it froze the shift. Daryll shuddered. With no human bodies, the Triumvirate would get away with murder. Again. "Nate needs to know this."

Zoe and the three Marston's nodded. When Daryll started to get up, Zoe closed her hand tighter over his. "He does, but we need to figure out some way out of this before we tell him. Please, Daryll. Give us tonight to work it out."

Daryll studied her eyes. "You're doing this to help the pack?"

"I am."

The truth of her words slammed into him, made him weak in the knees. His mate was helping to protect them.

"We all are." Peyton nodded when Daryll turned to look at him. "We're part of this, now. The Triumvirate lied to us, brainwashed us, made us commit atrocities for their twisted plans. We owe them retribution."

Daryll took a deep breath, then settled back into the booth bench and rested his forearms on the table. "I'm listening."

# Chapter 9

Kell sloughed off the glamour of age he wore the last several hundred years and strode silently through the heavily wooded ranch acreage. Soft step quiet, nose in the air, he followed a scent few would be able to trace. The prey he hunted wore at least one of the Ancient's medallions, making him impossible for most to sense or follow. Kell's soundless hunting steps grew closer and closer to his quarry. After slipping around and through briars and brush, he leaned his shoulder against a live oak tree's rough bark and watched his prey enjoying the sun.

Water warbled in the creek running past the flat limestone ledge the black wolf lay on. Soft summer winds breathed through overhead tree branches, rustling leaves and casting shifting shadows, marking the resting wolf, causing his fur to look almost blue when splotches of sunlight slipped through.

A dragonfly buzzed the wolf's ear, and it twitched. Birds twittered in the trees. Blue jays and red birds chased each other in the deep shadows beneath the trees lining the creek. Yawning, the wolf set his great head on crossed front paws and closed his eyes. Kell grinned, counted to fifty, then shimmered silently into a wolf. Paws silent, he crept closer. The only warning to the other wolf was the slight scrape of Kell's wolf's claws on the rock when he leaped at him.

Scrambling to a stand, the black wolf gave a deep-chested growl just before Kell's wolf slammed into him, entangling him in a rolling ball of paws and fur. Snarling, Kell snapped at the black wolf's neck. The two wolves rolled across the flat rock. Clawing and growling, they splashed into the shallow creek, then rolled apart. Facing each other, growls low in their throats, they stood in the water. When Kell's wolf stopped growling and shook in yipping laughter, the black wolf stopped growling and tilted his head, staring at him.

Kell's prey shimmered into human form standing in the ankle-deep water. "Shift!"

Kell's wolf growled, shaking his massive body when the Alpha command washed over him. He yipped and sat on his haunches in the water. Tongue hanging out, he studied the Alpha's surprised expression.

"Shift!" the Alpha commanded again.

Kell's wolf twitched his left ear to discourage the dragonfly that previously buzzed the Alpha's ear. When the Alpha blinked, a confused expression on his face, Kell grinned a wolfy grin, then shifted, laughing when the younger man blinked at him. "Your Alpha tricks don't work on me."

*****

Nate Rollins stared at Snarl, the oldest member of his brother's Arkansas Ozark Pack. Snarl looked to be in his ninety's last night. Somehow, today, the man didn't look a day over fifty. Raising his right hand to massage the tension from his neck, Nate frowned. "Snarl?"

"That'd be me, Son. My family called me Kell, but most know me as Snarl." He frowned. "You need to practice your skills. A real enemy would've gutted you by now."

Nate met Snarl's frown with one of his own. "What are you doing out here?"

"It's time to talk. There're things you need to know. Things that might keep you alive when you take your rightful place." The older man shrugged. "Or not. Most don't have the power to be..."

"Be what?"

"*Were* King, High King of the *Were* Council."

A shiver of anger burned across Nate's shoulders. "Who said I wanted to be *Were* King?"

Snarl frowned at him. "It's not a choice, Alpha. It's a birthright."

Standing straight, Nate crossed his arms and sucked air through his teeth. "You going to push me, too?"

"Push you?" Snarl sighed and motioned toward the boulders on the limestone ledge. "Sit down, Son. It's time you heard a few things."

Nate glanced down at the water they were standing in, then turned and waded to the creek bank. His clothes dripped water and his shoes made squishy slapping sounds as he walked to a boulder and sat down. He motioned for the older man to sit across from him on a facing rock. "You could have just come to the office where it would be more comfortable."

"Could've. Wanted to see something."

"What?"

"Wanted to see how alert you are. If I was a vamp, you'd be dead."

Nate studied the frown on Snarl's face. "I'm well-within my own pack territory. There's nothing here that can hurt me."

Snarl shook his head and shot a piercing look at Nate. "You going to tell yourself that when the vamps kill your mate and pup?"

Nate's spine snapped straight. His eyebrows lowered, threatening any who would harm his family. "What?"

Snarl held up his hand. "They're safe from me, Son." Snarl looked down for a moment, then raised his gaze to Nate. "You're about to become the most prominent shifter in the world. You, your family, and your pack must be ready, or none of you will survive it."

"You seem pretty sure of yourself."

"Seen it more than once. Five times…" His eyes lost focus as if he was seeing something afar off. "No, six times, since the last true *Were* King, I've seen Alphas strive for the crown." He brought his eyes into sharp focus and frowned again at Nate. "Six times I saw Alphas and their packs die. Don't want to see that again."

Snarl lifted his shoulders and spread his hands, palm up.

"Course, none of them was the true *Were* King. Didn't have the Royal lineage you have. Still, they died."

"And you know this first hand?"

The old man's face grew tight, a touch of turquoise showing in his eyes. "I do."

For some reason, Nate couldn't get a read on Snarl. Couldn't tell if he was telling the truth. Nate crossed his arms again. "Why should I trust you?"

"You got that newfangled Internet thing?"

"I do."

Snarl's jaw ticked, and his mouth quirked. Nate could see why the man was called Snarl. "Look up Thorkell Leifsson." He spelled the name out, letter by letter. "Thorkell Leifsson. Look it up."

"Why? Who's that?"

"That's me, Son. You won't find much, but I'm there. When you're ready to talk, no, when you're ready to listen, come see me." Annoyance in every move, the old man stood and walked briskly toward the ranch compound.

Nate raised an eyebrow, studying the retreating man's posture. "He doesn't move like an old man," he mused.

*He is Thorkell. His wolf is Snarl. Thorkell is the oldest living wolf. You should listen to him.* Koreth's thought surprised Nate. *Just how old is he?* He asked his wolf. *Older than some of the redwoods in California.* Left eyebrow climbing almost to his hairline, Nate tilted his head, watching the man everyone called Snarl stride out of sight, his back and shoulders as straight and strong as that of a much younger man.

# Chapter 10

When Snarl walked back into the house, Eli Thomas glanced at him. Sitting on the couch next to Renate, his wife, Eli studied the man standing over him. The old man was fuming, anger rolling off him in waves. Eli blinked. Snarl looked different. Younger. Eli's Alpha senses sharpened to alert. Exchanging glances with Renate, Eli stood up. "Snarl, what's wrong?"

For a moment, Snarl glared at Eli, then shook his head. "You're just as bad." He turned on his heel and stalked through the house, slamming the kitchen door as he left.

The front door opened, and Nate walked in. "Snarl in here?"

Eli waved toward the kitchen. "He just slammed the kitchen door on his way back out." He frowned at the annoyance in Nate's face. "What's up?"

"Don't know, yet. He jumped me out at the creek." Nate motioned toward his damp clothes and shoes. Even the Texas heat didn't completely dry him on his walk home. "Did you know an Alpha can't make him shift?"

Eli blinked and shook his head. "What happened?"

"I ordered him to shift to human. Twice. And he ignored it. Like I hadn't said anything." Nate's fingers combed through his wet hair. "How…?"

"I don't know, Nate."

Nate huffed and started for the stairs. "Let's go see what it is he wants us to know."

Eli followed Nate up the stairs, his lips twitching to grin at Nate's mutters. Since learning he was *were* and taking Jackson's medallions after their battle, Nate was 'top dog,' so to speak. Eli snickered at the thought, then sobered when Jabril, his wolf, informed him that the thought was insulting. Still, it amused him someone, anyone, especially someone as old as Snarl, could defy Nate. It was a new experience for his Alpha brother.

Nate slid into the chair behind his desk and pulled Janelle's laptop from the corner, opening it and powering it on. He drummed his left thumb on the desktop while waiting for the system to boot, then opened the browser. In the address bar, he typed 'Thorkell Leifsson' and pressed Enter.

Leaning over Nate's shoulder, Eli frowned at the search results. "Why did you search for a Viking?"

Nate clicked on the Wikipedia entry, read the first few paragraphs out loud, then looked at Eli. "Snarl said his name is Thorkell Leifsson."

Eli's eyes felt huge. He skimmed the information on the screen, picking up where Nate left off. "Leif Erikson's son. Wow, Snarl told me he was born in 1004, but I thought he was pulling my leg."

Nate stared at the screen for a moment, then looked over his shoulder at Eli. "He said my family and my pack will die if I'm not ready."

Eli jerked his gaze from the screen to Nate's eyes. "Die?" Eli studied Nate's fierce gaze.

Nate nodded. He glanced at the screen again, then shut the computer and stood up. "I think we better go see what he's talking about." Sucking air between his teeth, Nate frowned. "He said to come to see him when I was ready to listen."

"And you are? Ready to listen?"

Nate glanced at Eli. "According to Snarl, six Alphas have tried to claim the crown everyone keeps trying to force me to accept. They all died. Them and their families. I think I need to know more."

Eli took a deep breath. "I'm going with you."

"I hoped you would. Of all the *were*, I trust family the most. But I don't want our folks to worry unless it's necessary. Let's keep this between us for now."

Eli gave Nate a solemn nod. "Agreed. Let's go find Snarl."

When Nate walked out of the office, Eli was right behind him. No one was going to threaten his brother's family. Or his own, either.

*****

Nate stepped off the back porch and took a deep sniff. Identifying Snarl's scent, he followed the trail out of the compound and into the woods. Snarl, the wolf, was sunning in the same spot Nate enjoyed when Snarl attacked him. Old as he was, Snarl's coat was shiny, solid black, and full. The old wolf watched the two men walk up to him and sit on boulders. Nate twitched. His drying clothes were stiff and uncomfortable.

Knowing it was useless to try, Nate didn't tell Snarl to shift. Instead, he sat patiently on his boulder, waiting for the old man to decide to change. Snarl's eyes focused on Nate. For a moment, Nate felt Snarl try to place compulsion on him. Narrowing his eyes, Nate continued to stare at Snarl's eyes as they glowed turquoise. He felt Koreth close to the surface and knew his own eyes were glowing turquoise, too. Snarl's eyes faded back to brown. The wolf bowed to Nate, then shifted into Snarl.

"Good to know you can't be intimidated or coerced, Alpha."

"Mind telling me why you thought you should try?"

Nate's stomach muscles tensed when the old man laughed. "Afraid I want your pack, Son?"

When Nate didn't answer, the old werewolf laughed again and shrugged. "Might have, when I was a young pup, too stupid to know better." The old man chuckled and sat on a boulder facing Nate. His eyes lost focus for a moment. "No, I had my turn as Alpha. Didn't want it, then. Don't want it, now." He cleared his throat and turned his attention back to Nate.

Nate studied him for a minute. "So, you're Thorkell Ericsson."

Snarl gave him a half smile that didn't reach his eyes. "Everyone called me Kell, but Thorkell Ericsson is my birth name."

"Why do they call you Snarl, now?"

Snarl's forehead wrinkled, and he sighed. "When you're the son of a great Viking, *were* want to challenge just so they can say they did. I just got tired of fighting. Before I stepped down as Alpha, I commanded the pack to call me by my wolf's name, Snarl, so I wouldn't have to put up with it. Over the years, the old ones mostly died out or moved away, and the younger pups didn't know."

Snarl ducked his head. When he raised his gaze, the pain in his eyes hit Nate as a physical blow. Taking a sharp breath, Nate forced himself to sit firm and steady until the old man frowned, nodded, and looked down. "I'll tell you a story, Alpha." Snarl lifted his hands palm up toward his own face and stared at them. "These hands killed the last *Were* King."

Nate blinked at the words, then again at the shame and sadness that suffused Snarl's face. "I killed Eric the Red."

Nate leaned toward the old man, his voice gentle. "Why would you do that?"

"Because..." A sob tore the old man's voice. He took a deep breath and, tearless, gave Nate a sad smile. "Because she forced me to."

# Chapter 11

"Thorgunna, my step-mother, was human. She wanted my grandfather dead. Wanted me to kill him. She thought that my brother, Thorgils, as first-born, would inherit the pack and my grandfather's power, but Thorgils wasn't *were*. It was unusual, but he was born human." Thorkell bowed his head.

Nate opened his mouth to prod the man but snapped it shut when Snarl continued. "Thorgils was a strong man, a good man in battle, but he was... Thorgils was power hungry. Grandfather didn't trust Thorgils to put the *were* above himself. He forbade any to share blood with my brother to change him to *were*."

Thorkell shrugged. "I loved him. Without grandfather forbidding the exchange of blood, I would have been happy to do so, but when the Alpha King commands..." His eyes unfocused again and he took a heavy, painful breath then blew it out with force. "Erik the Red. My grandfather."

Nate scratched his ear and brushed away the dragonfly that still buzzed around them. He glanced at Eli. His brother watched Snarl, his eyebrows low on his forehead.

Thorkell took another deep breath. "Thorgunna threatened to kill my mate if I didn't do what she commanded. When I told Grandfather what she wanted me to do, he..." He looked down at his feet. "Grandfather told me to kill him. My grandmother died in a flood about a month before that. They were true mates. He was already slowly dying. He told me he wanted me to have his medallion and staff, and the only way to ensure I got both was for me to kill him and take them." Head still down, he shook his head. "I didn't want to. He was my..." His words softened to a whisper. "He was my grandfather. The only one in my family who really loved me."

Snarl looked at Nate, unshed tears in his eyes. "After I...after he was dead, I took the staff and the medallion that was mine by *were* right of birth. I found Freyja, my mate, and I left the village. We sailed for what's now called Canada and never returned."

Nate again glanced at Eli. Eli watched the old man, his face filled with compassion. Biting his lip, Nate turned back to Snarl. The old werewolf bent and picked up a live oak leaf from the rock near his feet, tore it into tiny pieces, and tossed the shreds into the creek.

"How old were you when this happened, Snarl?"

At Nate's soft question, Snarl looked up and lifted his lip into a snarl. "What does that matter? I was a man, and I killed him."

"How old?"

The old man let out a harsh sigh and shrugged. "I was sixteen that summer. Old enough to know better."

"But maybe not experienced enough to find a different way?" At the question, Snarl looked up with a frown. Nate motioned toward the compound. "Most of the wolves here are teenagers. Sometimes, they can't decide which movie to watch without input from others, much less determine a way out of the conundrum your step-mother put you in." Nate nodded. "You're right. You should have found another way, but evil people have been using teenagers for their own purposes since long before even you were born."

"I can't be trusted, Alpha."

Eli cleared his throat. "When I got to Arkansas, you welcomed me into the pack, stood behind me when others weren't happy I was there." Eli tilted his head and grinned at the old man. "You even gave me your Lycos' staff. Without it, I wouldn't have been able to focus my power. The Huntsmen might have killed someone."

"I never had a right to it. I didn't deserve the Lycos' staff, but it's not something you can give away if it doesn't want to go. It chooses the bearer. Over time, most forgot about the staff. Jackson learned of it when he found my journal."

Eli glanced at Nate, then looked back at Snarl. "You kept it for someone you felt you could trust. You prevented those who would have used it for evil from gaining it."

Snarl shrugged as if that wasn't important.

Nate realized that as *Were* King, the judgment of Snarl's actions would fall to him. He sighed, still resisting the responsibility everyone kept telling him belonged to him. "Where is Freyja now?"

"I don't know." A sob tore through the old man, and he shook his head. "I couldn't give the staff to Jackson. It can't be given unwillingly. Once it comes to a man's hands, it stays for life, unless it wants to leave. Jackson knew he couldn't force me to give it to him. He took Freyja and hid her somewhere. He promised not to hurt her if I wouldn't give the staff to anyone." Snarl bowed his head. "I don't even know if she lives."

"How long has she been gone?" Nate's quiet question brought the old man's gaze up.

"Fifteen years." The anguish the man felt crashed into Nate like a boulder. *An Alpha's emotions are dangerous*, he heard Janelle's words in his mind. When Eli gasped at the blow, Nate built a shield around himself and Eli.

Nate took the two steps necessary to reach the old man. Squatting, sitting on his heels, Nate clasped his right hand on the old man's shoulder. "We'll get her back, Snarl. She's your true mate. She's alive. We'll find her."

When the old man looked at him, Nate stared him in the eyes. "You've lived with the pain of killing your grandfather for too long. You've suffered your guilt for over a thousand years. That's worse than anything I could condemn you to. As the one you call *Were* King, I pardon you."

"I must be punished. I must."

The old man's anguish brought tears to Nate's own eyes, and he blinked to prevent them from falling. "Then your punishment is to be my aide. With your knowledge and experience at my side, reigning as *Were* King will be easier to manage."

Snarl took a deep breath and nodded. "I can do that." He looked at Eli. "Alpha, I request permission to move to the *Were* King's pack. I will take the position of aide, advisor, and bodyguard to the Crown."

Nate opened his mouth to object but closed it when Eli shook his head at him. Eli clasped Snarl's other shoulder. "You have my permission to leave the pack. Guard my brother well."

Eli grinned at Snarl and cut his eyes at Nate. "Even if he doesn't want you to, Snarl." Nate stood and frowned but didn't say anything.

The old wolf arose and bowed low to Nate. "My life and my service are yours, my King."

Looking from his brother to the old man, Nate shook his head. He studied Snarl, trying to find a diplomatic way to say no, but for the first time since he met the older werewolf, hope filled the man's expression as if he had a reason to live. He couldn't take that from the old wolf. Nate huffed. "I thought you were going to tell me what I need to know before I become the King."

"I am, Sire." When Nate rolled his eyes at him, amusement sparkled in Snarl's eyes. "The first thing you must learn is to accept your role. A reluctant king will be challenged. You are the *Were* King. It is your birthright. You must be willing to stand above the rest to keep them all safe."

Nate shook his head. "King." He sighed, doubt settling between his shoulders. "Not sure I can pull that one off."

Snarl nodded, his understanding of the road ahead in his eyes. "Just be yourself." He motioned toward Nate's chest. "To have access to the Lycos, you must wear the medallion. Be what you are."

"He has four."

Mouth open, Snarl blinked at Eli. "Four?"

Eli nodded and grinned as Snarl's expression changed. Nate grimaced when Snarl turned his amazed eyes toward the Alpha. "I had one. There was one here when I got here. I picked it up and they fused."

"And then you conquered Jackson in battle?"

Nate nodded at Snarl's statement. "Jackson had two. Before he died, the chains broke, and they fell off. I picked them up, and they fused to the first two."

Snarl shook his head bemused and sat on the boulder behind him as if he couldn't stand. "Four? It is forbidden to wear more than two." He looked up at Nate. "Seldom before Jackson have any worn more than one. The Ancients permit it?"

Nate nodded. He swallowed at the memory of the trial the Ancients put him through. After he offered to die to prevent his power as Lycos from destroying the world as he knew it, he blacked out. He believed at the time he would never wake. The Ancients surprised him when they trusted him enough to let him live. With four medallions, the Lycos' power... He sighed. "They gave me charge to protect all *were* and humans."

"Only one deemed worthy would be allowed to wear more than two." Snarl slipped off the boulder to his knees, his head bowed. "The Ancients have already named you the High *Were* King."

Nate rolled his shoulders, then rubbed the back of his neck. For some reason, the muscles in his neck were tight, painful. He looked at Eli and frowned at his brother's shrug. "Okay, Snarl, stand up. If you think this is what the Ancients wanted, I'll do my best, but I don't want you bowing to me."

He tilted his head and watched the spry old man stand. "Why do they call you Snarl, anyway?"

Snarl's eyebrow lifted. "How many people you know named Thorkell?"

Nate snickered. "Good point. How about Mr. Thorkell? They don't have to know it's your given name."

Snarl grinned and shook his head. "If you don't mind, Sire, I'd just as soon stay Snarl. It's my wolf's name, and it gives the young ones reason to leave me alone."

Nate laughed. "Fair enough. I'll call you Snarl if you'll call me Nate."

"I'll call you whatever you command, Sire."

A loud clanging rang out across the ranch. Nate glanced toward the compound, then grinned at Snarl. "That's the dinner bell. Let's go eat. And Snarl?"

The old man raised an eyebrow. "Sire?"

"Call me Nate." Nate grinned at the old man's dry chuckle, then turned and led the way back to the picnic shelter where everyone gathered for their meal.

# Chapter 12

Nate led Snarl and Eli around the corner of the shed, heading for the picnic shelter. The teens, werepanthers, werebears, and werewolves were playing a game of football in the compound yard. Nate heard Adrian, one of the werepanther teens, shout. He turned to look just as Snarl growled, snagged the teen from the air, and slammed him to the ground. The teen lay perfectly still, his startled eyes staring up at the old werewolf, a football tucked against his chest.

Nate caught Snarl's fist before it pummeled the boy and pulled him away from Adrian. "What are you doing?"

"He attacked you!" Snarl kept a threatening gaze locked on the boy.

Nate frowned and looked down at Adrian. Still on his back, caution in his expression, Adrian stayed where he was, unmoving, watching the old man Nate held by the arm. "Are you hurt, Adrian?"

Eyes wide, his gaze still on the old werewolf, the teen gave a slight shake of the head. Nate released Snarl and reached down to give the boy a hand up. Adrian allowed his Alpha to pull him to his feet but maneuvered to make sure Nate was between him and Snarl. Nate glanced past Adrian and saw the other boys running toward them. He realized Snarl was growling and put his hand up to stop their advance.

He turned to look at Snarl. "It's okay, Snarl. They were only playing football."

"I tried to stop, Alpha." Adrian shook his head. "I was looking back at the quarterback. By the time I saw you, I couldn't stop. I yelled so maybe you could get out of the way."

When Nate nodded, Snarl's growls stopped. "I'll talk to Jonathan, and we'll come up with a better place to play ball."

"Yes, Sir." Adrian cut his eyes at Snarl, then blinked and looked back at Nate. "Can we go?"

"Put the ball away and come eat."

"Yes, Sir." Adrian walked away, but not before glancing again at the old werewolf beside Nate.

When the boys were out of hearing range, Nate chuckled. "Didn't know you could move that fast, Snarl."

Snarl frowned, his gaze searching Nate's expression. "I thought he was attacking you."

"Right now, there's no one here that would do that, but it's good to know you're keeping watch. You'll have to show me that move, sometime." Nate clapped the old man on the shoulder and noticed for the first time the corded muscle hidden beneath the man's clothes. Eyebrow raised, he turned and walked to the shelter. The smell of flame-grilled burgers filled the air.

One of the werepanther women approached, her hands clasped at her waist. "I'm sorry, Nate."

"Not a problem, Dottie. Adrian's okay, just a little shook up." He smiled at her and turned toward the barbecue grill.

Jonathan finished turning the burgers and shut the grill. "I'll get the boys to mow the pasture on the other side of the fish tank for football if you like."

"That's a good idea. This afternoon too soon?"

"No, I'll make assignments as soon as everyone eats."

"Sounds good, Jonathan." Nate glanced at the teens walking toward the picnic shelter. "The compound yard is a little close to the houses for football."

Jonathan nodded and waved toward one of the front tables. "The food is all set out. I only have a few more burger patties to finish up."

Nate picked up a plate, started making his hamburger, then turned to look at Jonathan. "Oh, I want to have an Alpha Council meeting at 4 p.m. Let everyone know, will you?"

Busy, Jonathan nodded without looking around. Nate motioned for Snarl and Eli to fill their plates. Nate and Eli sat at one of the tables. Snarl pulled a folding chair over against the one solid wall of the shelter and sat down, facing Nate, the wall at his back. Nate raised an eyebrow and glanced at Eli. When Eli shrugged, Nate decided to eat now and ask later.

Half an hour later, Snarl followed Nate up the stairs in the main house to the office. When Nate sat in his executive's chair, Snarl walked past him and stood with his back again against the wall, facing the room. Nate swiveled his chair to face the old man and frowned. "Have a seat, Snarl. We need to talk."

Snarl frowned. "I can protect you better if I stay here."

"I'm sure that's true. However, there is nothing endangering me, right now, and I want to talk with you." Nate indicated the chair next to him. "Please."

With a stiff nod, Snarl took the seat. "You have questions."

"I do. First, how could you move that fast? You had Adrian on the ground before I even knew you moved."

Snarl looked at Nate, then glanced past him out the window. "I trained as..." After a hesitation, he sighed and looked at his hands. "After I left my father's people, Freyja and I traveled. We went to Canada. There was no reason to stay there. Freyja wasn't happy, so we went to Europe. We wandered across several countries, never staying in one place more than five or ten years."

Red touched the old man's cheeks. "Gregorio di Montelongo, the Patriarch of Aquileia, saw me shift, named me a demon, and decreed my death. With Freyja's help, I escaped prison in Venice. When Marco Polo went to Asia, we went with him."

Snarl wiped his mouth with his right hand and frowned. "I learned martial arts in China. When Marco went back to Europe, we stayed behind with a family of weretigers. They had their own fighting form. I learned the assassin's art from them."

He shook his head when Nate caught his breath. "No, I never killed for them, but I learned. After that, we spent a few years with werefoxes in Korea. When Germany started strutting, I realized World War I was coming."

Snarl wet his lips and glanced at Nate. "I'm no coward, but I'd already seen so much war...so much killing. I brought Freyja to the United States. We found the Arkansas Ozark Pack and stayed with them. When their Alpha died in a forest fire, his daughter asked me to take the Alpha role until a male heir was born. Because she was a Royal, I agreed. I became Alpha until the previous Alpha's great-grandson was born. I gave him my medallion, and we, Freyja and I, retired. His grandson was Grant and Jackson's father, your grandfather."

"What about Dusty? Did you know Jackson had him chained in the cellar?"

Snarl looked at Nate for several long seconds before he nodded. "Dusty would only let me give him the wire he used to get free when Jackson was gone. He wouldn't even let me teach him to use it to pick the locks on the manacles. He insisted on teaching himself. Said he didn't have anything else to do. When I could, I brought him food, and I made sure he had blankets when it was cold. I offered to free him, but he refused. Dusty said Jackson would follow him to you if he left."

Snarl cleared his throat and looked down, his words full of his regret. "He refused to escape."

# Chapter 13

Nate studied the old wolf. Snarl's story matched the little he knew of his parents and grandparents. He glanced at the wall clock. The Alpha Council would gather in two hours, and he still needed information. Nate leaned back in his chair, but he didn't know the right questions. "Tell me what I need to know, Snarl."

"To reign as the *Were* King, the *were* Alphas, all *were* Alphas, must accept you. Werewolves, werepanthers, werebears, werefoxes, werelions, and more. You will need to invite their Alphas to the *Were* Council. Some will accept you without question. Others may force you to prove yourself, first.

"Prove myself how?"

"Until you show them you are the One True-Blood Royal Lycos, they will not accept you. And only then if you can force them to."

"Force them?"

Snarl nodded. "The One True-Blood Royal will have the power of Alpha Command over all *were*. Only he can command the Alphas of the different packs, dens, etc."

Nate frowned, thinking of his attempt to force Snarl to shift. "But not over you?"

"I'm a Royal Alpha, too, Nate, but I don't have your honor." Regret haunted his eyes. "I could never be the *Were* King. My wolf..." Snarl looked out the window and shook his head. "My wolf won't allow it. As Lycos, you would have the ability to give me Alpha Command, but without the Lycos' power..."

"So, when I'm human, you and I are equals. That it?"

"Blood equals. The medallions give you more power than I have." Snarl cleared his throat and shuddered. "I don't want the power. It's too much."

*Me, either.* Nate sighed when Koreth huffed at his thought. "So, as far as the Alphas, I just need to give them an Alpha

Command?"

Leaning forward, Snarl crossed his forearms on the conference table. "If that was all, it wouldn't be difficult. Even if challenged, you would win."

"But?"

"What do you know of the V-Triumph?"

"Not enough." Nate tilted his head. "But you obviously know more."

"During the Dark Ages in Europe, vampires rebelling against the Ancients formed the Venerati, who eventually became V-Triumph. The Venerati organized the Black Forest Huntsmen, a group of humans dedicated to the hunting and destruction of *were*. The humans are not told their masters and leaders are vampires. All *werekind* were targets, but with the Lycos being of wolf descent, wolves became the major targets. Over the years, the Huntsmen lost track of other shifters."

Snarl's eyes became unfocused again. "Gregorio di Montelongo, known to history as the Patriarch of Aquileia, was the first Huntsman in Venice. I intended to kill him for the shifter deaths he caused, but Freyja begged me to just leave. I couldn't ignore the fear in her eyes, so we went to Asia."

He blinked, his gaze focusing on Nate. "I told you I've seen six try to take the crown. Six times, the Venerati attacked. Six times, they won. They brought Huntsmen to the Council Conventions to stop the coronation. Most present died, including the families and packs of the Alphas who laid claim to the throne. Now, they call themselves V-Triumph. They will attack again when the call for a Council Convention goes out. They can't stand against a true Royal *Were* King with a united *were* behind them. Their only hope is to destroy you before you ascend the throne."

"How did you escape the attacks?"

Snarl raised his gaze to Nate's intent stare, shame deepening the red in his expression. "For Freyja's sake, I ran. I took her and ran. We were massively outnumbered. At least a hundred to one.

Maybe more. One shifter wouldn't make a difference."

"And this time?" Nate's thumb beat a staccato rhythm on the table. "Will we be outnumbered by so much, and will you run this time?"

"No." Snarl sat straight in his chair, met the Alpha's stare. "You have pardoned me my crimes. I owe you my future. Whatever the numbers, I will stay and fight for you."

Nate's thumb stopped its beat. "Even if we find Freyja?"

"Even if." Snarl swallowed hard. "I've spent my life preparing to fight for the High King, hoping I could earn a pardon." He blinked and swallowed again. "I feared to die before... I didn't deserve..." He shook his head. It was odd to see a man so old look like a lost child. "I could never go to Valhalla with my Freyja if..." He hung his head. The tick of the wall clock was loud in the room. "There were none I believed could stand against V-Triumph until I met you."

"Snarl, look at me." When the old man looked up, Nate searched his eyes. "I believe you. All that was long before I was born. I've already pardoned you for your grandfather's death. These events are forgotten and will not be brought up again unless you think there is something I need to know."

"My life is yours, Sire, to use as you will."

Koreth caught back the retort that pushed against Nate's lips. He didn't want that responsibility, either, but it seemed fate had more in store for him. At Koreth's insistence, Nate nodded. "I accept your pledge of loyalty and fealty. However,..." He made sure the old man was looking at him. "I'm capable of protecting myself. As my self-appointed bodyguard, I want you to promise to protect my mate and child if, or when, fighting starts."

"But..." Snarl broke off when Nate raised his hand.

"I can't fight if they are not safe. From what you've told me, and what I saw when you thought Adrian was attacking me, you are the best man to keep them safe. Your job is to protect them if I am engaged elsewhere."

"Yes, Sire."

71

Snarl's words released the tight knots in Nate's neck and shoulders. Since the first time the crown of the *Were* King was brought up, he worried over Janelle's and Ophelia's safety. He wasn't sure why the old man's acceptance eased his concern, but it did. "Thank you."

The old werewolf gave him a solemn nod.

Taking a deep breath, Nate considered all he had heard. "If I call the packs a few at a time, will the vampires attack?"

"No, they'll wait until all have been called to the Council Convention for the coronation, so all can witness your destruction."

Nate steepled his hands over his chest, fingers spread wide, leaned back in his chair, stared at the ceiling. He tapped his thumbs together while he thought. After a moment, he sat up and frowned. "If I call, say, only the werebear Alphas to the ranch, will V-Triumph attack?"

"No, Sire. They'll wait until the Council Convention."

"That's what we'll do, then. I'll call each species' Alphas to the ranch at separate times. After I meet with each, only then will I send a call for the Council Convention."

Snarl thought about Nate's statement, then nodded. "That would let you get past claiming your rights before the convention started. It might work. The vampires will still come, but the convention would be united against them."

"Good. Since there are werebears and werepanthers here already, I'll have them come first." Nate blew out a loud breath. "In the meantime, I'll contact the general again and see if his vampires can help."

"The general?"

"A group of vampires and shifters has been working within the human system to try to keep the V-Triumph group controlled. General Brighton is the commander of the group in the United States."

"Humph. Never heard of such."

Nate smiled at Snarl's obvious distrust. "General Brighton

was my commanding officer in the Marines. I think I can persuade him to bring the Elites to the ranch for backup."

"You trust him?"

"I do."

"Then, unless he gives me a reason otherwise, I'll trust him, too, Sire."

"I thought you were going to call me Nate."

The old man looked sheepish. "I'm trying."

Nate laughed, then sobered. "Well, if you can't, at least call me 'sir.' I don't want to answer questions 'sire' will bring, yet."

# Chapter 14

Nate and Snarl discussed the best way to assemble the *were* Alphas until the Alpha Council started coming in, taking their seats at the conference table. Snarl stood and moved to stand at the wall. Nate glanced at him, then ignored him. The old man insisted on guarding him, even when Nate believed it wasn't necessary.

Nate asked Koreth to call Daryll Crane, the leader of the pack werebears, to the meeting. When Daryll tapped on the office door and stepped in, Nate motioned him to an empty seat at the table. Counting Snarl, there were thirteen individuals from his pack in the room, five born werewolves, three changeling werewolves, three werepanthers, one werebear, and one human. In addition to his own council members, Eli, the Arkansas Ozark Pack Alpha, and his mate Renate were also in attendance, bringing the number to fifteen.

With a double-knock on the conference table, Nate called the meeting to order. "We have a lot to discuss and prepare for, so let's get started." With a glance at Daryll, Nate leaned forward, elbows on the table and looked at Janelle. "Record that Daryll Crane was offered a seat on the Alpha Council and accepted." Janelle smiled and added the note to the meeting journal.

Nate glanced around the table at all the faces. At Snarl's previous request, Nate kept the origin of the information confidential. "When I call the Council Convention, I believe the V-Triumph will attack. The Venerati, the previous version of V-Triumph, organized the Black Forest Huntsmen to destroy *were*, so they would have no one to keep the vamps from enslaving and breeding humans for food."

Daryll blinked, the pallor of his face paling. "Food?"

Nate nodded, not surprised at the werebear's reaction. "V-Triumph vampires prefer human blood to that of food animals.

From the beginning, the Ancients gave charge to the *were* to protect humans from the vampires. The Venerati organized the Black Forest Huntsmen and have used them to decimate the *were* population over the past nine centuries."

Nate frowned when Daryll glanced at Marston. Colonel Marston sat stiff and straight, his clasped hands resting on the table. The fine tremors in the former Huntsman's hands and his strained expression brought Nate's eyebrows low over his eyes. "During that time, six times an Alpha tried to take the *Were* King position. Each time, Huntsmen attacked the Council Convention. Each time, the Alpha trying to gain the crown and his entire pack died. I'm working on a plan to prevent that happening again."

"Nate?"

Marston's quiet voice brought Nate's gaze back to the former Huntsman. "I didn't know about the vampires until...until ..." Marston took a deep breath and tried again. "They lied to us. We were told we were defending humans against *were*. That *were* wanted to destroy humans." Marston glanced at Daryll. "Paige, Phillip, Zoe, and I want to help you stop them. We have a plan to get some intel for you."

# Chapter 15

The office was so quiet Nate could hear the mowers beyond the fishing pond where the teens worked to build their ballpark. Moving only his eyes, Nate looked around the table at each member of the Alpha Council. All were studying the former Colonel. Nate flicked his gaze to Marston. "What do you have in mind?"

Marston took a deep breath. "First, Zoe has family still in the Huntsmen. We would like the opportunity to get them out, to try to convince them to join us." He glanced at Daryll.

When Daryll nodded encouragement to Marston, Nate frowned. "Go on."

"Daryll has offered to work with us. We want permission to leave the ranch to locate and retrieve Zoe's aunt. She..." Marston looked uncomfortable. Nate frowned at the tinge of fear he smelled coming from him. Marston took another breath, squared his shoulders, and retreated into military bearing. "Zoe's aunt has been monitoring your ranch finances for more than a year. She siphons off minuscule amounts into an account that supports her clandestine activities against the pack."

Nate raised an eyebrow and looked at Janelle. Janelle bit her lip and nodded. "There's been a discrepancy in the books for most of the past two years. We've lost nearly four-hundred-thousand dollars. I've been searching for it, but we've got numerous accounts, and it never comes from the same account more than once. That makes it hard to find." She looked at Marston. "Can you give me her account information?"

Marston shook his head. "The only person who could do that would be Gisele Schneider, Zoe's aunt. Zoe, Daryll, Paige, and I would like permission to bring her here. I know Gisele. I believe she would be horrified at the V-Triumph and their objectives."

"I'll consider it. Anything else?"

At Nate's question, Marston again glanced at Daryll. "Daryll told me Zoe informed you the locators are in our rings. I'm not sure if she told you the rings have a spring-loaded needle in them. If we remove them, we are injected with a fast-acting poison. Daryll and Zoe think they've figured out how to remove them safely, but I want them to remove mine first."

"Why yours?"

"I'm a wolf, now. My metabolism may help me survive the poison if it can't be removed without triggering the needle."

Nate looked from Marston to Daryll. "You have a way?"

Daryll cleared his throat. "You know Bess makes jewelry?"

Nate nodded. "She gave Janelle a copper cuff soon after you moved here."

"Bess still has some of the sheet metal she used for the cuff. I think we can use a narrow piece of it to remove the rings." Daryll shook his head, a frown between his eyebrows. "I won't let them test it on Zoe."

Nate frowned at the intensity of Darcel's silent agreement with Daryll's statement. He glanced at Marston. "But you're willing to be the test subject, Colonel?"

"Peyton." The former Huntsman gave Nate a half-grin. "I'm not a colonel, anymore, and there are three of us named Marston."

"Okay, Peyton. Answer the question."

"Yes, Sir. I volunteer to attempt to remove the ring using Daryll's idea." He spread his hands apart, palm up. "We can't leave the ranch while we are still wearing the rings. If we do, the Huntsmen can follow us. Once we take them off, the locators will stop working. They have a kinetic spring, similar to some watches so that they don't have to have a battery."

"And once they are off?"

"Once we remove them, after a couple of hours, the Triumvirate will likely assume we're dead. For that reason, if no other, Zoe's should be removed last since she was sent here to kill all of us. I think they'll believe she killed us, and maybe you, and the *were* killed her in revenge."

Nate tapped his thumb against the table. "You've given this a lot of thought."

"We all, Zoe, Phillip, Paige, and I, want to stop the Triumvirate, Alpha. Once the Triumvirate thinks we are dead, they'll notify Gisele and Maria, Zoe's mother, that we've been killed in the line of duty. They may even send them to avenge us. Even if they don't, I believe Maria will come to Gisele. I'd like to be in Corpus Christi, waiting for Maria to arrive. We could bring them here, then remove their rings. Again, the Triumvirate should assume they came here to kill and were killed in the act."

"And if they won't work with you?"

The pain in Peyton's eyes fed his bleak expression. "Zoe thinks they will, but if not, she will accept your judgment of them."

Nate glanced at Daryll, and Daryll nodded. "Zoe's worried about them, but she understands the evil in the Triumvirate. She will accept whatever judgment you give."

Janelle caught Nate's left hand, bringing the thumping to his attention.

Nate stilled his thumb and glanced at Janelle's raised eyebrow with a sheepish grin. "Sorry." When she smiled back, he turned back to the Council. "Okay. Any objections to Daryll's and Peyton's idea?"

No one spoke, and most shook their heads. "You have my permission to remove the rings. I want Dottie and Ben there. They're the closest thing we have to healers, right now." Nate glanced at Peyton. "If the poison injects, you may need them. I'll decide on the rest of it after you get your ring off."

Nate cleared his throat. "Now, I called this meeting to discuss which *were* group's Alphas to invite to the ranch, first."

The meeting continued until Nate realized he was too worried about Zoe and the Marston's to pay close attention. Adjourning for the evening, Nate asked Ben to pick up Dottie and go to Daryll's house. Nate and Janelle walked with Daryll back to his house. Marston took a detour to go pick up Phillip and Paige to bring them to Daryll's, too.

When Daryll led Nate and Janelle into the house, Bess looked up from the table, surprise in her eyes. "Nate!" She stood fast enough she knocked over a vial of beads into a shallow tray. Glancing at the beads covering the design she was working on, she sighed, then moved the tray aside. "Would you like some coffee or tea?"

"Thank you, no." Nate looked around the living room and kitchen. He regretted not visiting before. "Is Zoe here?"

"She had a bit of a headache come on, so I gave her some acetaminophen and sent her to bed. Would you like me to see if she's still awake?"

"I'll check on her." Daryll walked to the bedroom door, tapped twice then walked in and shut the door behind him. Nate could hear him murmuring to Zoe. A moment later, the door opened, and Zoe walked out, hand-in-hand with Daryll.

When the doorbell rang, Daryll nodded at Bess. "That's the Marston's."

Bess nodded, went to the door, and welcomed the three to the house. Daryll cleared his throat. "Bess, you still have a little of that plate copper, don't you?"

"The jewelry metal? Yes." She glanced around the room and swallowed. "Was there something wrong with the bracelet I gave you, Janelle?"

"Oh, no, Bess. It's lovely." Janelle sent a quick glance at Nate. When he nodded, she turned back to Bess. "We were wondering if we could borrow it for a few minutes. It might be what we need to remove the locator rings the Marston's and Zoe are wearing."

Bess' stress level dropped. "Oh. Sure. It's on the table in my satchel." She walked to the table, opened a leather pouch, and pulled out two small pieces of thin copper plating. When she turned with it in her hands, the doorbell rang again.

Daryll opened the door and let in Ben and Dottie. Dottie carried her apothecary case with her. Daryll motioned toward the table. "Let's clear off the table, Bess. They're going to need lots of light, and that's where the best lighting is."

Bess nodded, and with Daryll's help, quickly cleared her beading supplies off the table. Daryll sat and motioned for Peyton Marston to sit next to him. While the rest watched, Daryll took the thin plate metal, bent it into a slight curve, then starting from the wrist side of Peyton's finger, Daryll slowly slid the metal beneath the ring until it came through the other side. Then, pulling the sheet of metal with it, Daryll eased the ring off Marston's finger. Daryll and Peyton both jumped when the needle pinged against the sheet metal.

Daryll removed the sheet metal. An ugly green stain spread slowly across the curved copper. Peyton held up his hand and showed it to the crowd. "It worked."

Bess pulled a paper cup from the cabinet and Daryll dropped the ring inside. Daryll reached for a paper towel to wipe off the sheet metal for the next use.

Dottie gasped. "No. Don't."

Nate turned to Dottie. "What?"

"Can't you smell the Wolfsbane in the poison?"

Surprised, Nate turned back toward the ring and sniffed. *Wolfsbane?* Nate could smell a faint odor that made him nauseous. The smell was covered up with another acrid smell, but it was there. He shook his head. "So?"

Dottie swallowed. "Nate, ingestion by humans, or an injection, would probably intensify the toxin in the other poison, but even the touch of Wolfsbane that strong on the skin can kill a werewolf."

Without a word, Daryll dropped the scrap of metal in the cup with the ring. "We can't use this again, Bess. Do you have more?"

Bess nodded and handed him the second of the two pieces. "I have another sheet of it in my bedroom."

Daryll looked at her, his face grim. "Bring it, and the metal snips. We'll have to have a separate piece for each of the other three rings."

"Bess."

Bess stopped and looked at Nate. "Yes, Sir?"

"Order twelve dozen sheets. Hopefully, we'll need them for other Huntsmen. Whatever we have left, you can have for your jewelry business. If we use it all, we'll order more for you. Give the invoice to Janelle. She'll reimburse you for the expense."

"Yes, Sir." Bess hurried out of the room to get her last sheet.

While Bess was gone, Daryll used the piece in his hands to remove Phillip's ring. Expecting the ping of metal on metal, he didn't jump when the needle discharged. As soon as the ring was off, he dropped the ring and the small metal sheet into the same paper cup.

Once Bess returned, Daryll snipped two small pieces of copper off the sheet, curved them, then used one of the pieces to remove Paige's ring. At Nate's suggestion, they waited an hour before removing Zoe's ring.

*Maybe, the Triumvirate will believe she came after me after she supposedly killed the Marston's.*

# Chapter 16

Zoe sat in the back of the RV, buckled into the table bench next to Daryll, playing poker. Daryll took a look at his hand, folded, then watched while Zoe raised Paige and Phillip. Both met her raise, and Phillip called. Daryll laughed at the playful pout Zoe sent her friend when Phillip dropped an ace-high royal flush on the table and raked the pile of pennies into the bowl that held the rest of his winnings.

"I win." Phillip gave Zoe a smug grin, then motioned toward the bowl of pennies. "I'll give half my earnings for a sandwich."

Paige elbowed him. "Silly. All the pennies belong to Dad."

"Well, yeah, but I don't think he would want his only son to starve."

Peyton's voice came from the driver's seat of the RV. "Think again, Son. I want those pennies back."

Phillip wrinkled his nose and shook his head. "Guess I'll have to starve, then. I'm fresh out of cash."

Paige laughed and unbuckled her belt. She walked to the small refrigerator and removed sandwich makings. Setting them on the table, she opened the cabinet and pulled out a stack of paper plates, counted out five, then put the rest away. She slid back onto the bench beside Phillip, buckled her seatbelt, and started preparing sandwiches for them all.

"Don't forget the chips," her dad called.

"I'll get them." Daryll unbuckled, retrieved the chips, then sat again.

When the sandwiches were made, Paige handed a plate to Phillip for him to hand to their dad, then handed each of the others a plate. Zoe gathered all the pennies they used for their poker game into a small plastic container, sealed it, and placed it behind the rail on the shelf over her head.

Daryll took a bite of his sandwich and watched Phillip and Paige banter about who would win the next poker game. He cut his eyes at Zoe and grinned at the smile on her face. She seemed to be over the dizziness from her injury. And she was more relaxed since the former Huntsmen's rings were removed. Daryll finished his sandwich and chips and tossed his plate into the trash can strapped to the wall beside the door. "I'm going to see if Peyton needs a break, so he can eat."

He winked at Zoe, then grinned when her face reddened. Sliding out of the table bench, he walked to the front of the RV, slid into the passenger's seat and buckled the seat belt. "You need a relief driver?"

Marston waved his half-eaten sandwich in the air. "Almost done. I'm fine." He glanced at Daryll and grinned. "Phillip won again, huh?"

"Yeah."

Marston threw a quick glance over his shoulder, then whispered low enough the humans in the back wouldn't hear him. "The boy cheats."

Daryll laughed. "I know. He's pretty good. It took me a while to catch on."

Marston grinned. "He only cheats when he's playing with my pennies, though. Never when he's playing for keeps."

Daryll snickered and glanced out the front windshield. "Be much longer?"

"Just about there. Our exit is coming up in a couple of miles."

When Marston didn't continue, Daryll looked at him. "Worried?"

"Well, yeah. Justin, Zoe's dad, was killed in a Huntsman raid last year. Maria's been pretty rabid against the *were* since. Then Zoe's sister died this year in France." Red tinged Peyton's face. He glanced at the passenger side wing mirror, flipped on the right turn signal, then smoothly moved into the right lane. "I'm worried she might not listen, before getting violent." Peyton shot a quick glance at Daryll then turned back to his driving. "She'll be armed with silver."

Daryll sighed. "I expected as much. I'm not as allergic as you are, though, so you should probably stay toward the back. Silver stings me. It burns you."

"Yeah." Marston swallowed the last bit of his sandwich. "I'm worried she'll try to kill Zoe before she understands."

A low growl erupted from Daryll's chest. At the wry look Peyton sent him, he shrugged. "Darcel and I both get a little hot-headed where Zoe is concerned."

"I noticed." He quirked an eyebrow at Daryll. "Are you allergic to Wolfsbane, too?"

"Nope. Werebears don't have the same weaknesses, or at least not to the same extent, that werewolves have. Silver stings, and if there's very much of it, Wolfsbane stinks and fills the nose so it's hard to smell anything else. I was surprised Dottie smelled it on your ring before I did."

"Dottie seems to know a lot about herbs and medicines."

"She does." Daryll tilted his head and studied Peyton. "You know Ben is courting her, right?"

"Really? Not a clue." Peyton cut a quick look at him. "Dottie's sweet, but I'm not interested."

"That's probably a good thing. Nate doesn't like mate challenges."

Peyton choked, jerking the steering wheel, then correcting his course with a competent hand. "Does Ben think I want to challenge for her?"

"Nah. I just wanted to pull your chain." Daryll grinned at the annoyance in Peyton's rolled eyes. Daryll's eyes narrowed. "But there is someone you're interested in."

Peyton looked in the rearview mirror to see if his kids were listening. Daryll's gaze followed Peyton's. Paige and Phillip were arguing over who got the last can of Dr. Pepper, totally oblivious to the conversation in the front. "Maybe." Peyton's muttered word was too low for the humans to hear.

Flipping the turn signal, Peyton eased onto the exit ramp. Daryll grinned at the man's flushed face. "I take it Paige and Phillip don't know."

"No. They don't. And they won't. Nothing is going to happen."

Daryll suppressed Darcel's rumble of anger. "Because she's *were?*"

"Because she doesn't want another mate."

"Another mate?" Daryll thought over the *were* on the ranch, then his right eyebrow climbed almost to his hairline. "Nettie? Are you talking about Nettie?" he hissed.

Peyton ignored him. "We'll be there in about two minutes." At his call, the passengers in the back quietened down.

Zoe unbuckled her belt and walked toward the front of the RV as they turned onto a residential street. "That's it. The tan house at the end of the street." She took a sudden breath. "And that's Mom's car out front."

Peyton drove past the house and turned right at the corner. Two houses past Gisele's he pulled the RV to the curb and parked. Blowing out a breath, he looked over his shoulder at Zoe. "Show time."

# Chapter 17

Daryll walked to the front door of Gisele's house, the others close behind. The front drapes were closed tight, so he was confident his small group hadn't been seen. Glancing back to make sure Zoe and the others were out of sight behind him, Daryll slipped his left hand into his pocket to prevent them seeing he didn't wear the signet ring, then pressed the doorbell. Footsteps walked to the door, then the door opened. A small forty-something woman with the same color blonde hair as Zoe's stood in the open door, looking up at the huge man she found on her doorstep.

"Yes?"

Daryll gave her a tight smile. "Ms. Gisele Schneider?"

"Yes?" Her eyes narrowed as she looked him up and down. "Do I know you?"

"No, Ma'am. I'm here about your niece." He stuck his right hand out. "I'm Daryll."

She looked at his hand, then looked back at his face. "You'll have to excuse me, Mr., uh, Daryll. My niece passed away recently." She swallowed and started to shut the door.

Daryll's foot stopped the door, and she looked at him. He kept his voice pleasant but fused it with Command Voice. "Let me come in."

Gisele blinked, her struggle to disobey causing her to twitch.

"Let me come in." When Daryll repeated the command, she opened the door wide.

"Please, come in."

Daryll stepped in just as a strained voice called from the kitchen. "Who is it, Gisele?"

"I'm a friend," Daryll told her.

"A friend," called Gisele. She stepped back for Daryll to come in, then her eyes widened in fear when Zoe, Paige, Peyton,

86

and Phillip followed him. She gasped and whirled.

Daryll caught her arm. "Stay here and stay quiet." When his command hit her, she stopped, but her fear-filled gaze darted from him to Zoe, and then back.

Peyton closed the door behind him. Daryll pulled Gisele into the living room and gently pushed her into a recliner. "Don't say or do anything to alarm Maria. Call her to come in here."

Daryll watched her internal struggle against his Command Voice. "Call her."

"Maria? Come in here."

"Let me get the quiche out of the oven."

The door to the oven squeaked open. A pan scraped across the oven's wire rack, then plopped onto the stovetop. The oven door banged shut. The smell of eggs, bacon, and onion wafted into the room from the kitchen. Maria walked around the corner, pulling off her oven mitts.

"What is...?" She stopped, her eyes panic wide. Her voice dropped to a whisper. "Zoe."

"Mom." Zoe took a step toward her mother, her hands reaching out.

Maria squealed and whipped around. She took three running steps before Daryll's command stopped her. "Come in here. Stay calm."

Visibly fighting the command, Maria walked into the living room. Daryll pointed toward the second recliner. "Sit there and listen. Both of you listen."

Peyton harrumphed. "What was that?"

"Command Voice. All Alpha's have it."

Zoe jerked to face him. "You're an Alpha?"

Daryll sighed. "I'm the Alpha to my group."

"Did you hurt them, Daryll?"

"Of course not, Zoe. They're your family. I could only hurt them if they tried to hurt you. I used Command Voice to prevent that. Darcel and I can't let anything happen to you."

Zoe started to turn toward her mother, then turned back.

Her lips pressed tight, and she scowled at him. "You used that on me!"

"Only to keep you from hurting yourself. You were injured, and you wouldn't stop fighting." Daryll ran his large hand over his face. "Only the first night, when I took you to the hospital, Zoe. I promise."

"Not since then?"

"Not even once."

Peyton harrumphed. "This isn't really the time for a lover's quarrel."

Daryll turned and took a step toward Peyton, a growl sounding deep in his chest.

Peyton put up both hands, palm out. "Sorry. I shouldn't have interfered. I just thought we should get done what we need to do and get back."

Zoe caught his arm. "Stop, Daryll. He's right. This isn't the time." She glanced at her mother and aunt. "Or place."

Pulling an ottoman away from a rocker, she sat facing the two women. "First, I'm not dead. And I'm not a wolf."

"How can we know that?" Fear shook Maria's voice. "The werewolves always..."

"No, Mom, they don't." Zoe turned and waved a hand at Peyton. "Peyton's the only wolf here. And he's only a wolf because I nearly killed him."

Both women shrank back from Peyton. Gisele turned her gaze to Zoe. "You changed him?"

"I couldn't. I'm not a wolf, Aunt Gisele." When shame colored Zoe's face, Daryll put a comforting hand on her shoulder. "I...I tried to gut him, and I..." Zoe shook her head, unable to continue.

"And she did a good job of it." Peyton stepped closer. "The Alpha knew I wouldn't live long enough to get to the hospital. He gave me the option. Live as a wolf or die of my wounds. My kids were there. I had to live to make sure they were alright."

"You *chose* to become an abomination?" Maria's words

dripped with disgust.

"I chose to live. I chose to stay with my kids. I chose to fight vampires instead of the wolves dedicated to saving humans."

Marie shook her head. "What? There are no vampires."

"Yes, Mom. There are. The three members of the Triumvirate are vampires. They organized the Huntsmen centuries ago to hunt and destroy the only hope humanity has. They want to use us like cattle. To breed us as stock."

Maria blinked and slowly shook her head. "I don't believe it." She glared at Daryll. "Release me from your control."

"So, you can kill Zoe?"

"What?"

"I can feel the compulsion the Triumvirate put on you to kill any who have been alone with the *were*. I can't remove it, but I can feel it. To some extent, I can control it."

Maria glared at him. "Those who've been alone with *were* are compromised. They have to die to protect the Huntsmen!"

Zoe bowed her head, then looked up at Daryll. "See, I told you. They'll kill me if they can. All of us."

Daryll squeezed her shoulder. "We'll take them to the ranch. Nate can help them, just as he helped you."

"By turning her?"

Sighing, Daryll looked into the furious face of his soon to be mother-in-law. "No, Maria. By saving her." He looked at Gisele. "We need information about the funds you've been siphoning off the ranch accounts."

Gisele's face paled. "I didn't..."

"Don't lie, Gisele. I can smell a lie. All *were* can."

She glared at Zoe. "You said only Peyton was a wolf."

"And she told the truth. I'm not a wolf." He tilted his head and watched her. "I'm a bear."

Gisele laughed. "And you accuse me of lying?"

Daryll shimmered into Darcel. The grizzly hunched over to keep his ears from brushing the ceiling and growled. Both women gasped. Daryll shimmered back into himself. "I'm a

89

bear."

The two women cut their eyes at each other. Both paled even more. Gisele swallowed. "I didn't know there were werebears, too."

"Truth. You told the truth, that time. There is much you must learn about the *were*. Zoe hasn't learned it all, yet, either. For now, we need your account information, and Zoe and Paige will be searching you for weapons." He stepped back to let the two girls get closer. Zoe moved to her aunt, unable to bear the glare in her mother's eyes.

Maria frowned. "Zoe, how could you. Wolves killed your father. And he," she pointed at Peyton, "killed your sister."

"I did." Peyton bowed his head. "And I'll live with it for the rest of my unnaturally long life."

"Mom, Lana begged him to kill her. She believed what we were told, that she would turn because she was bitten by a wolf."

"What?" Maria looked at Zoe. "She was bitten?"

"When they attacked a wolf family, she was bitten in the attack. She begged Peyton to kill her." Zoe swallowed, and tears streamed down her face. "She believed the lies, too."

"What lies?"

"That wolf bites turn humans into werewolves."

"Oh, Zoe." Maria's voice softened. "Zoe, honey, that's true."

Peyton shook his head. "I wasn't bitten, Maria, but I'm a wolf. It just doesn't work that way."

"Then how?"

"A blood exchange. You have to take in the wolf's blood and he has to take in yours." Peyton sighed. "The Alpha took my blood and gave me his so that I could survive Zoe's attack."

"Why didn't you kill him, Zoe?"

"I tried. If not for the Alpha, I would have. I tried to kill the Alpha, too. But I was injured. The Alpha sent me to the hospital for treatment. They aren't evil, Mom. They aren't."

Gisele cleared her throat. "So, are you only here for the

books?"

"No, Aunt Gisele. We want to convince you that you've been brain-washed. That the grand plan to save humanity is actually a devious plot to destroy us." Zoe looked from her aunt to her mother. "Please understand. I need you to go with us. You'll be so surprised to learn the *were* are good people. Most of them are kind and caring."

Maria shook her head, tears in her eyes. "They've brainwashed you."

"No. They helped me see the truth." Zoe wiped tears from her mother's face. "We're taking you with us. Back to the ranch."

"No." Fear in the word, Maria shook her head. "No. Not tonight."

Zoe frowned. "Why? Why not tonight?"

"Not tonight." Maria clenched her jaws and pressed her lips together. She shook her head, eyes full of fear.

Zoe studied her mom, then looked at Gisele's terrified expression. She bit her lip and looked at Daryll. "Something's wrong. Make them tell us what's going on, Daryll."

The werebear studied Zoe's face. "Are you sure? So far, I've only been holding them in place so we could talk to them. Forcing them to talk will be a greater violation."

Maria sobbed. Daryll glanced at her, then back to Zoe. Zoe nodded. "Something's wrong. Something's... Do it, Daryll."

"Okay." Daryll turned to Maria. He sighed, centered himself, and used Command Voice. "Maria, you will answer Zoe's question fully and without leaving anything important out."

"No." Maria was shaking with the effort to defy him.

Daryll looked at Zoe again. "Are you sure?"

She swallowed, nodded, then whispered, "Yes."

The thought that Zoe might later regret this terrified Daryll, but when he looked at Maria, then Gisele, he knew she was right. Daryll stepped past Zoe, pressed his hand to Maria's forehead. "I command you to speak." The Alpha command resonated throughout the room.

Maria sobbed. "The Huntsmen...the Huntsmen are..."

Zoe gasped. "It's the full moon! The Huntsmen think the wolves have to shift under a full moon. They're attacking the ranch tonight, Daryll." She hugged herself and whispered, "The children."

Before Zoe finished speaking, Daryll pulled his phone from his pocket and called Nate's number.

"Hello?"

"Nate, the Huntsmen are coming tonight!"

Nate cursed. "Are you sure?"

"Yeah. Zoe's mom just let it slip."

"How many?"

Daryll looked at Maria. "How many?"

She shook her head, her lips pressed together. Daryll looked at Zoe. "I'm sorry, Zoe. We have to know." Zoe blinked but didn't answer. Daryll pressed his hand to Maria's forehead. Instead of waiting for her to answer him, he swept into her mind, his bear's clawed toes clicking as they walked through the corridors of her memories. When he pulled out, Maria moaned and sagged against Gisele, eyes closed.

"Nate, there're at least five squads on the way, maybe more. They don't know about the bears or panthers." Gisele's startled jerk brought Daryll's gaze to her. "The plan is to surround the compound and all attack at once when the first wolves start shifting. They intend to kill with silver while wolves are shifted." He listened for a moment. "Yeah, we're on our way back. We're bringing Maria and Gisele with us. The Huntsmen will kill them if they find out we were here." Daryll nodded. "Yes, Sir. We'll be careful."

Daryll disconnected the call. He pulled two small pieces of curved metal from his pocket and used them to protect the two women's hands while he removed their rings and tossed them on the coffee table. He glanced at the Marston's. "Search the house. Anything that looks like a weapon, bank records, or computer equipment goes with us."

Peyton nodded and motioned Paige and Phillip to follow him. Daryll turned to Zoe. She sat with her eyes clenched shut, her shoulders shaking. Ignoring Gisele, Daryll dropped to his knees in front of Zoe. He gently raised her face. "Zoe." She opened her eyes at his whisper. "I'm so sorry, Zoe. I didn't want to do that."

Zoe sniffed, nodded, and sniffed again. "I know. I'm sorry you needed to."

"We'll get through this, Honeysuckle. I promise."

"I know, it's just... She's my mom, Daryll." She caught a shaking breath and sobbed. "She's my mom."

He caught her face in his hands. "I am so sorry, Zoe. I'll spend my life making it up to her. Making it up to you. I swear it, Zoe. I swear it."

# Chapter 18

*Janelle, where is Eli?*

Janelle blinked and turned toward the kitchen door, even knowing Nate was upstairs in the office. *He's on the front porch with Curtis.*

Nate's feet thundered down the stairs. Janelle stepped from the kitchen to the hall and watched him jump the last four steps of the stairs, then swivel toward the front door.

"What's wrong, Nate?"

"Huntsmen are coming. Get the kids in the saferoom!"

Before Janelle could process the thought, he ran out the front door, the door slamming behind him. Janelle frowned. *We need to have one of those hydraulic door closer things to keep the door from slamming so often.* Then what he said brought her up short. *Huntsmen!*

Memories of the massacre jumped into her mind. All the dead. All the blood. Janelle gasped and pushed them away. No time for things that couldn't be changed. Rushing out the back door, she used the cast iron dinner bell hanging on the back porch to send the alarm sequence throughout the ranch. Before the last peal of the bell quieted, children from across the ranch were running toward the main house, their parents right behind them.

As children streamed into the house and through the cellar door to the safe room, Snarl appeared at her elbow. Janelle nodded an acknowledgment to the ancient wolf, then rushed inside toward the stairs. She stopped as she saw Cynthia, her mother-in-law, carrying Ophelia down the steps, a diaper bag draped over one shoulder.

With the children safe inside and Ophelia safe in Cynthia's arms, Janelle glanced out the front windows. Nate, Eli, Renate, Jonathan, Ben, Flora, Will, Curtis, Don, and the two human soldiers stationed on the ranch were standing together in the center of the yard talking while the rest of the adults and all the older teens gathered around them.

Wishing she could be with them to face the coming threat, Janelle sighed and motioned for Cynthia to precede her into the basement. Janelle's job was to care for and protect the children. Before the massacre, Randall, her brother and Alpha, didn't allow women to train to fight. In front of her, Cynthia moved Ophelia to her left shoulder and stepped onto the basement steps. Janelle followed, with Snarl close behind. After everyone was in the safe room, Snarl turned and shoved the heavy, steel door closed. The snap of the locks engaging echoed in the narrow stairwell.

The whisper of Snarl's footsteps on the stairs behind Janelle raised the hair on the back of her neck. Even for a werewolf, the man was unnaturally quiet in his movements. At the bottom of the stairs, Janelle clapped to get the attention of the five adults and twenty-four kids. The kids ranged from four-weeks-old to thirteen, with only four younger than five-years-old.

"Quiet." Janelle's soft word silenced all but Ophelia, who was beginning to fuss for her afternoon feeding. "We are safe here, so there's no reason to be afraid."

Mattie's wide eyes stared up at her, her thumb in her mouth. The child tugged on the hem of Janelle's blouse. When Janelle looked down at her, the six-year-old pulled her thumb out and whispered, "Alpha protects?"

"Alpha will protect. Don't be afraid." Janelle gave the girl a smile more confident than she felt and gently stroked the girl's hair. She motioned toward the shelves lining the back of the room. "There are colors, coloring books, and lots of games and toys on the shelves. You older kids find something to keep you busy."

Dottie and Nettie set up playpens for the three babies, then set the two older babies inside with their toys and a small blanket. The soft voices of playing children hummed through the room.

Forcing herself not to bite her lips, Janelle glanced at Snarl. The old man stood at the bottom of the stairs, his back to the children. If someone other than pack came down the stairs, he would stop them or die trying. Taking a slow deep breath, Janelle looked at Cynthia and smiled.

Cynthia glanced at the stairs. Her eyebrows lowered over her eyes, her forehead wrinkled. "How do we know what's going on?"

"Koreth will let us know anything we need to know." Janelle pulled a clean bottle out of the diaper bag, added formula powder, poured in liquid from a gallon of purified water, then shook the bottle to dissolve the powder. She would nurse Ophelia later, but right now, the children needed to eat, too.

"Lily, would you like to feed Ophelia while we get lunch prepared?"

Thirteen-year-old Lily was one of Janelle's best helpers and often babysat when Janelle was working in the office. The panther girl grinned and nodded. After she sat in the only rocker in the cellar, she took Ophelia from Janelle and offered the bottle to the fussy baby. Ophelia latched onto the bottle nipple, then made faces when she found formula instead of breast milk. After mildly fussing, she finally settled and suckled. Lily laughed. "Guess you were hungry, Princess!"

After getting the babies and toddlers set, Dottie turned to Janelle. "Need help in the kitchen?"

Janelle smiled agreement at Dottie and glanced at Cynthia. With a tight nod toward the small kitchenette the bear carpenters built into the corner, she walked to the cabinets and started perusing the contents. The freezer was full of easily prepared foods, and the cabinets filled with non-perishable canned and boxed goods. Six weeks' worth. Nadrai growled in the back of Janelle's mind. *We won't be here that long.* Janelle shook her head. *No, we won't,* she agreed with her wolf.

"Let's make some mac and cheese with boiled weenies for the kids." Janelle pulled boxes from the shelves, set them on the counter, and found a can of condensed milk. She pulled a pound of butter from the freezer. Dottie found two 5-quart pots below the counter, filled them with water, and set both on the stove. While Janelle and Cynthia opened boxes, Dottie opened six packages of weenies and put them in water to boil. Once the weenies were cooking, Dottie opened the canned milk, poured it into a pitcher and added water.

A few minutes later, Ophelia finished her bottle. Lily burped her, then put her in the playpen Dottie set up for her. Soon, all the babies had been fed and put down for naps. The older kids each had a disposable bowl of mac and cheese with diced weenies stirred into the macaroni. Not the most nutritious meal, but right now taking care of hunger was more important.

While the kids ate, Janelle listened, trying to hear what might be happening upstairs. Nothing. She swallowed and stood to organize the cleanup. Soon the children were again playing, drawing, coloring, or reading.

An hour later, Janelle wondered if it was a false alarm when a thought cloaked enough to keep from upsetting the children broke through. *They come!* She stumbled and caught herself against the kitchenette counter, fear for her mate and pack shivering through her.

# Chapter 19

The trip back to the ranch was strained. With two women as prisoners, two laptops, a desktop computer, four hard drives, three USB drives, two ledgers, and three large cardboard boxes full of weapons and silver ammunition they confiscated, the RV was crowded. Maria and Gisele were buckled at the back of the u-bench surrounding the table. With Zoe on the verge of a panic attack, Daryll asked Peyton to drive the return trip, too.

He sat beside Zoe, his arm cuddling her close to him, while she rocked in a short backward and forward motion, her arms wrapped around her midriff as if she were afraid she would come to pieces if she let go. Darcel whimpered, afraid Daryll's earlier actions would drive her away from him. Daryll was more concerned for her vacant gaze.

"Zoe."

She didn't respond.

"Zoe. Sweetheart, look at me." Still, she rocked. Daryll sighed and stroked the hair away from her eyes. "Sweetheart, I'm sorry."

Finally, slowly, she raised her gaze to him. "Don't ever do that again."

"I won't. I promise."

She nodded, but the rocking continued. Darcel's heartbroken whine worked its way out Daryll's mouth. Zoe stopped and looked at him. Really looked at him, for the first time since they left Corpus Christi. "I told you to...to..."

"She'll be okay, Zoe. Dottie and Nate can fix it."

"Are you sure?"

"If Dottie can't, Nate can. He helped you, remember?"

Zoe blinked, then nodded, her gaze trapped in his. She sniffed. "What if they hurt the children? What if the Hunters hurt Ophelia?" She sobbed. "What will Nate do if they hurt Ophelia?"

Daryll swallowed. "I don't know, but it won't happen. Nate won't let it happen. He's much more powerful than you know."

"Is he?"

"Zoe, Nate is the most powerful shifter on Earth. He won't let anything happen to the children, to Ophelia." Daryll's thumb brushed tears from her cheek. "I promise. Nate can protect them all. All by himself, if he has to."

Her hand came up to brush his eyebrow. "You really believe that."

"I do. I was there when Jackson challenged him. I saw a fraction of what he can do. He's even more powerful now than he was then. If the Huntsmen attack, they will be in more danger than the kids are."

Zoe sighed and bowed her head again. "Give me Alpha command, Daryll."

Daryll glanced at Paige's worried eyes, then looked down at Zoe again. "What?"

"Give me Alpha command. Tell me to be strong. Tell me to stop being afraid. Tell me to be ready to fight."

Daryll groaned and bowed his head. "You don't know what you're asking, Zoe."

"Please, Daryll."

"I can't." Daryll shook his head and looked at her. He leaned forward and kissed her forehead. "I won't."

"Why not?"

"Because if I do, you'll never know. You'll always wonder if whatever happens tonight happens because it just happened that way, or if I forced you to take risks you wouldn't normally take. Zoe, the only time I used a command on you was to make you sit still so you wouldn't aggravate your head wound. That was before I...before I fell in love with you." He stroked her cheeks with his thumbs. "I couldn't do what you ask and live with myself. I love you too much."

She tried to pull away, but he held her still. "Zoe, you are strong without false strength. You are brave without false bravery."

"You really believe that?"

He nodded and pressed a kiss to her forehead, then leaned back to look at her. "Even before Darcel wanted to claim you, I was impressed with your bravery against all odds. Not many *were* would have the guts to attack the Alpha with a knife, but you did. You did, and you lived. To my knowledge, you are the only one who ever attacked Nate after he became Alpha that lived."

When doubt showed in her expression, Daryll tilted his head and smiled at her. "Peyton, you hearing this?"

Peyton's voice came from the driver's seat. "Yep!"

"Am I telling the truth?"

"Yep! Every word."

Daryll released her face, picked up her hands, then kissed each of her fingers. "See. I'm telling the truth. I'll always tell you the truth, Zoe. Always."

Her gaze searched his eyes. Her face softened, losing its rigid pain, relaxing. She pulled his hands to her and kissed his knuckles. "I love you, Daryll Crane." She sniffed and swallowed. "I love you."

He picked her up, set her on his lap, and held her against him the rest of the two-hour trip. He glanced at her mom and aunt. Her mother's face was slack as if she wasn't really there. Her aunt watched his interaction with Zoe, no sign of her emotion on her face.

After Zoe sighed and went to sleep, Gisele cleared her throat. "What happened to her?"

"When she attacked Nate after stabbing Peyton, the Alpha backhanded her away from him. She fell against a log post. At the hospital, they stitched her head wound and told me she had a concussion. She's not quite over it." Daryll shook his head. "I shouldn't have brought her, but she was so worried for you both... I just couldn't tell her no."

"When you were on the phone with your Alpha, you said we didn't know about bears and panthers."

"There are several dozen werebears, and almost that many werepanthers on the ranch."

Gisele's gaze moved to the girl in his arms. "She loves you."

Daryll blinked. "Tonight is the first time she said so."

Gisele looked at her sister-in-law. "Just what did you do to Maria, anyway?"

Misery flooded Daryll. "I walked through her mind when she didn't want me to."

"You can do that?" When Daryll didn't answer, Gisele nodded. "Of course, you can. That's the only way you could have learned about the attack tonight."

He sighed. "I didn't want to. It hurt Zoe. I'd do anything to keep from hurting her."

"So, what's going to happen to us? Me and Maria?"

"That's up to Nate, but if you're willing to listen, you'll learn the truth about the Triumvirate."

"And that is?"

"You didn't believe it the first time. Why would you believe it now?"

"Ah. Good point." She glanced past him at Paige, then past her to Phillip. Phillip rode in the passenger seat up front, next to his dad. "Paige and Phillip haven't been changed?"

"No." Daryll shrugged. "Since their dad was, if they choose to change, Nate might allow it, but they have to want it and they have to ask."

Gisele rubbed her left arm from elbow to shoulder, then down to her elbow.

"Are you cold?"

She seemed surprised. "A little."

"Sorry about that. Shifters are hot natured, so we like it really cold." He glanced at Paige. "Do you have a blanket Gisele can use?"

*****

101

Paige nodded. "There's one on the bed." She walked to the back of the RV and opened a door. A moment later, she was back with a soft blanket and draped it around both Gisele and Maria.

"If you're still human, why do you stay with them?"

Paige looked at her. "I've been with them as long as Zoe has. Phillip for longer." She shrugged and grinned. "At first, I was scared. Everything the Triumvirate taught me kept running through my mind, but when I watched, I found what the Triumvirate said didn't jive with what I saw. Instead of a group of animals always at each other's throats and fighting in the street to kill anyone who crossed them, I saw a group of people who cared for each other. They work together, play together, and eat together."

Paige glanced at Daryll. "They've treated Zoe with kid gloves, even though she almost killed Dad and tried to kill their Alpha. They understand what we've been taught and are willing to work with us to let us see the truth."

Paige grinned at her Dad's back and saw him grin back at her in the rearview mirror. He looked younger every day. Before long, he would look young enough to be her brother. *That'll be strange.* Paige sighed. "Dad would've died if Nate hadn't changed him to wolf. It almost didn't work. I thought he was going to die. While Nate was trying to save Dad, he promised Dad that he would take care of me and Phillip if Dad didn't make it."

Paige looked down. For long moments, she stared at one of the boxes holding weapons found in Gisele's house. She picked up a compound crossbow, then picked up a quiver of silver quarrels and slung it over her back. "We're almost there."

"Who are you hunting, Paige?"

Paige looked at Gisele. "I'm not hunting. I'm protecting. Friends, family, innocent children, and babies." She took a deep breath and let it out in a rush. "I won't stand idly by and watch them be slaughtered."

"You'll fight your friends."

"No, Gisele. I'll fight my enemies. I know who the

102

Triumvirate are. If I can help it, I won't let them succeed."

"Neither will I." Paige looked at Zoe. Sometime during Paige's conversation with Gisele, Zoe woke up.

Zoe squirmed out of Daryll's lap, then stood and reached into the box for another compound crossbow and quiver of quarrels. Then she picked up a set of throwing knives and hid them inside her clothes. "I won't let them hurt Ophelia. I don't want to kill them, but if it's the only way." Zoe looked at her aunt. "If it's the only way to keep Ophelia safe, I will."

Gisele frowned. "Who is Ophelia?"

"The Alpha's baby girl." Paige located another dagger in a leather scabbard in the box.

A sound somewhere between a purr and a hum filled Daryll's chest. Paige glanced at him in time to see him grin at Zoe. "Darcel said you are the best mate ever."

Zoe nodded and smiled. "That's the plan."

Paige felt like she was intruding on a private moment and turned away, embarrassed. She finished buckling her belt and checked that the dagger was snapped into the scabbard. Paige looked up and saw Gisele's attention fixed on her. The older woman pursed her lips but didn't speak. Paige took a deep breath and let it out slowly. *Dad's a wolf and my best friend is mating a bear?* She shook her head and wondered how much weirder things would get before it was all over.

# Chapter 20

Ten minutes before they arrived at the ranch entrance, two helicopters flew overhead. Daryll glanced out the window and frowned. It was too dark to see anything but the lights on the copters. "Looks like they're headed toward the airstrip."

"You have an airstrip?" Gisele's voice betrayed her surprise.

Daryll looked at Gisele. "And a plane, and a copter. You've had access to our financials and didn't know?"

"Bank records don't always specify what money is spent on, just where it is spent."

After thinking about that, Daryll nodded. "Suppose so." He looked out the window and frowned at the vans, SUVs, and Jeeps parked alongside the county road. "Looks like your friends are here."

"Should I drive onto the ranch, Daryll?" Peyton's gaze met Daryll's in the rearview mirror. "They may start shooting."

Daryll frowned. His mate and her family were in the RV. He couldn't allow them to be targeted. "Go to the back entrance and let's see if we can surprise them."

Peyton nodded and drove past the ranch entrance. Ten miles later, he turned left on a county road just past a bend in the road, drove another eight miles and turned into the back entrance. He stopped the RV and looked at Daryll.

Daryll nodded. "Turn off the motor. I'll see what's going on." Slipping out the RV door, Daryll ran into the woods. Shimmering into a bear, Darcel stood on his hind legs, listening and sniffing the air. With a snort, Darcel ran toward the bear compound, then stopped at the edge of the clearing where the werebear's houses were located. All the lights were off in the houses. No one was home. He sniffed again, then nodded. All the bears were shifted and waiting among the trees around the main house for the Huntsmen to attack.

A motor sounded, and a Jeep crested the low hill. General Brighton stood in the passenger's seat, scanning the clearing through binoculars. Behind him, six more Jeeps followed. Daryll stepped out of the woods and waved. Brighton turned and said something to his driver. A moment later, the Jeep stopped in front of Darcel.

The General jumped out. "What's happening?"

Darcel shimmered into Daryll. He ignored the General's barked question. "How many men did you bring? Are they...?"

"*Were*? If not, they're vamps. I don't bring humans into a paranormal battle." Brighton tilted his head. "There's twenty-five of us. More waiting for a call, if they're needed. What's happened?"

"I haven't been in touch with Nate. Huntsman vehicles are lining the county road at the ranch entrance. I'm not sure how many Hunters there are. We were told it would be at least five squads, maybe more." Daryll grinned. "Our one big advantage is the Huntsmen don't know there are *were* other than wolves."

"Huh. That's good news." He shook his head. "Come to think of it, all *were* but the wolves have been off vampire radar for centuries." He grinned and turned to his men. "Dismount, men. You're going *were!*"

Men jumped from every vehicle, setting their weapons inside and shimmering into their animals. Daryll watched the elite soldiers in Brighton's command shimmer into lions, leopards, tigers, wolves, and foxes. Only six men, the drivers, remained in the Jeeps. When Daryll raised an eyebrow, Brighton grinned. "The rest are vampires. All have vowed to stop the V-Triumph. With their lives, if necessary."

Daryll nodded and pointed toward the main compound. "There will be bears, panthers, and wolves in the compound, as well as a few humans under Nate's protection. If he can, he'll keep the humans out of the battle, so they won't be confused for Huntsmen."

Brighton nodded. "We'll be on our way, then. Where are

you going?"

"Back to my group. They're waiting about a mile back in an RV for me to return. We'll be there soon." Daryll turned away, then turned back. "I have four humans in the RV, General. They must be protected. Do not allow your soldiers to harm them."

"Understood."

Daryll nodded and shimmered into his grizzly. As the soldiers' *were* animals faded into the wooded acres, Darcel rushed back the way he came. In the distance, he heard scattered rifle fire. Surprisingly little of it, with what he knew was happening at the compound. He frowned. *Most of the Huntsmen must be armed with crossbows.* No more gunfire than there was, if the neighbors even heard the commotion, they probably thought someone was hunting javelinas. Nothing else was in season.

Running at top speed, it took less than three minutes to get back to the RV. All the lights were out. Darcel stopped and sniffed to make sure there were no unexpected surprises between him and the RV, then shimmered into Daryll and walked to the door. The interior light briefly flashed like a beacon when he entered the RV, then shut back off after the door closed behind him.

"What's out there?" asked Peyton.

"I don't know how many Huntsmen. Brighton brought five squads of his soldiers. Most are *were* and shifted to filter through the trees. Six are vamps." Daryll sighed. He still hadn't figured out what to do with his prisoners during the coming battle.

Peyton buckled a belt loaded with knives and grenades around his waist. "Why don't Paige and Phillip stay here with Zoe's mom and aunt, while the rest of us see what we can do to help?"

Daryll looked at Zoe to see what she thought of Peyton's suggestion. Zoe nodded, but before she could speak, Gisele said, "No." Hands flat on the table in front of her, Gisele leaned forward. "Leave Zoe here."

Daryll studied the woman's face. To his werebear eyes, they

106

were as clear to him as in full daylight. "Why?"

"The Huntsmen know she was supposed to have died. They'll believe she's *were*. Even if they don't, they'll try to kill her, just for being alive."

Daryll's eyes cut toward Zoe. She raised her head and looked at him. "I won't stay here. If you're going, I'm going."

Darcel's gruff, happy growl startled Daryll. *Our mate is brave! Worthy to birth bears.* Daryll sighed. "I don't want you in danger, Zoe."

She shook her head. "Doesn't matter where I am. Tonight, danger's everywhere. I want to be with you."

# Chapter 21

When Daryll, Peyton, and Zoe moved toward the RV door, Phillip caught Zoe's arm. "Wait."

Zoe shushed Daryll's low growl, then looked at Phillip. "What?"

Phillip pulled a clean camouflage-patterned bandana from his pocket. "The moon will light your blonde hair up like a lamp. Cover it with this."

Daryll huffed and nodded. "He's right. Cover up."

Zoe took the bandana, folded it into a triangle and used it as a scarf to cover her hair. Rather than tie it beneath her hair at the back of her neck, she tied it under her chin, so it was less likely to fall off if a branch caught it. "Better?"

Daryll nodded. "Better. It'll make it harder for humans to see you."

"But not *were*?"

She loved the grin Daryll gave her. "Most *were* can see in the dark, Zoe. Better than humans can, anyway."

"How are we going to get there, Daryll?" Peyton motioned toward Zoe. "She can't keep up if we go *were*."

She watched Daryll tilt his head and consider the question. "Do you have any rope or straps?"

Peyton started to shake his head, then smiled. "There was a roll of nylon rope in one of the boxes of weapons we found in Gisele's garage."

Daryll walked to the first box, searched through the contents, then moved to another. Zoe frowned. "What are you doing?"

He stood and showed her a spool of heavy nylon rope. "Making a harness so you can ride."

"Ride what?"

"Me." Daryll grinned at the incredulous look she sent him.

"Darcel, I mean. And if you're riding behind me, it means my hands, um, paws will be free for fighting, and you'll have some protection."

"So, you plan to be a human, or bear, shield?"

"Yep." He pulled off yards of the rope and started knotting it to make a harness to fit over his bear's shoulders and back.

She shook her head, fear clutching her middle. "I don't like using you for a shield, Daryll."

"And I don't like you in danger. We'll be moving too fast for you to keep up. Ride or stay here."

"I can run."

"Fifty miles an hour, or more?"

"What? You can run that fast?"

"My bear can. So, can Peyton."

Zoe sighed and motioned toward the rope. "If I have to ride to go with you, I'll ride."

Daryll snickered and continued tying the rope. "You'll have to put it on me after I shift, otherwise it'll go with my clothes." He finished the harness. "Let's go."

Zoe nodded, sent a quick glance to her mother and aunt. Her mother's face was still blank, while Gisele bit her lips, her eyes tight with worry. Sighing, Zoe followed Daryll out the door. She watched Daryll pull a rifle strap over his shoulder then shimmer into Darcel. Darcel sat on his haunches. When Zoe couldn't reach high enough to slip the harness over his front paws, Peyton took over and put the harness on Darcel, then tied the hanging rope ends across the bear's stomach.

Peyton caught Zoe by the waist and lifted her high enough to slip her feet into the loops Daryll tied in the rope. She caught the loops on either side of Darcel's neck and wrapped them around her hands to keep from slipping out.

Darcel made an inquisitive sound, not quite a growl. Peyton nodded at the bear. "The straps will hold. She's okay."

"You can understand his bear?"

Peyton glanced up at her. Sitting in the harness on Darcel's back, her head was two feet higher than Peyton's. "I can. I think it's a shifter thing."

Zoe stroked the fur between Darcel's ears. "Well, let's go. The fight will be over before we even get there."

Darcel roared and took off running. Zoe shivered at the speed the bear attained, wondering how he could be running so fast. A flutter of movement at her side brought her head around, and she grinned at the sight of the large gray wolf loping beside her bear.

Running through the trees instead of staying with the road, Darcel soon passed the bear's homes and ran toward the main ranch compound. Zoe could tell he was avoiding low hanging branches as best he could, but an occasional branch stung her cheeks when they charged past them. When gunshots again echoed in the darkness, Darcel sped up. Ducking her head to protect her eyes and face, she didn't see the branch that struck her head.

Zoe moaned, the pain in her head growing, burgeoning into a full migraine. Beneath her thighs, she felt Darcel's distressed rumble, and shook her head, trying to push away the faintness swamping her. When Darcel came to an abrupt stop, only the straps Zoe wrapped around her wrists kept her from flying off the bear's back.

Darcel dropped to his haunches. Still unable to see past the pain, Zoe felt Peyton's hands on her waist, holding her up as Darcel shimmered into Daryll. Too loose to stay around the much smaller man, the rope harness fell off Daryll. He stepped out of it, then turned and gently unwound the straps from Zoe's wrists and ankles. Dropping the rope to the grass, he took Zoe in his arms and sat cross-legged on the ground, holding her in his lap.

"Zoe?" His gentle fingers lifted her head.

She blinked several times, then groaned. "I can't see, Daryll. I'm dizzy, and I can't see."

The werebear muttered a curse. "I think her concussion...

110

Can you go on without me, Peyton?"

"Yeah. What are you going to do?"

"I'm taking her to the cave. She needs to rest." A deep, sorrowful moan rattled his chest. "I didn't see the branch, Zoe. I was watching the muzzle flashes and didn't see it. I'm sorry."

"It's okay." Having her eyes open and seeing nothing frightened her. She closed her eyes, then felt as if she was sinking into the darkness. "Daryll..."

\*\*\*\*\*

Daryll didn't see the branch, but he felt the jar when it slammed into Zoe. As fast as he was running, there's no way it didn't cause severe damage to her healing head. A dark spot grew on the bandana Zoe wore over her head, and he smelled the iron and copper tang of blood.

Angry with himself for his carelessness, he looked at Peyton. "From here on, stay human. The Huntsmen will want to kill you as a wolf, so they won't have to dispose of a human body." He glanced at Zoe, then looked up. "Do you want my rifle?"

"No." Peyton patted the pistol holstered on his belt. "I have a weapon, and you might need the rifle."

Daryll nodded. "Be careful." He stood, cradled Zoe in his arms, and ran toward the caves. As a human, he couldn't run as fast as his bear could, but Darcel was afraid his claws might injure Zoe more and refused to shift. Behind him, Daryll heard the soft, almost inaudible sounds of Peyton running toward the main house.

It took Daryll three long minutes to run to the cave. His chest grew tight, his breath harsh as his fear grew. Zoe, barely over the concussion from her fall, was a dead weight in his arms. The same spot on her head was injured again. Stopping in the trees by the creek, he listened and sniffed. Good. No one was here. He waded the creek, stooped to get in the low entrance, and carried her into the cave Nate and Janelle found the teen wolves

111

hiding in when Janelle first brought the Alpha to the ranch. The cot Jonathan used while recuperating from silver poisoned wounds was still there, a blanket folded neatly on the foot.

Daryll laid Zoe on the cot, elevated her feet with the blanket, then carefully untied the knot holding the bandana on her head. It was already soaked with blood. Though he could see well enough in the moonlit woods, the darker interior of the cave made seeing her wound difficult. He left her long enough to pull brush over the cave opening. Thankful the cave was maintained as a haven for emergencies, he lit the Coleman lamp and hoped the bend in the cave entrance would shield the light from the Huntsmen.

Darcel's anguished moan rumbled in his chest when he turned to look at Zoe. There was more blood in her hair than there was the day he took her to the hospital. He set the lamp on a crate close to her. Opening her eyelids, he checked her pupils. They were unequal in size and unresponsive to the light. His sensitive hearing caught the faint flutter of her heartbeat. It was weak and thready. While he listened, her heart beat slower and slower. The slower her heartbeat, the more his terror grew.

She was dying. And it was his fault. Daryll released a single sob, then did the only thing he knew to do. He shifted his right hand into a bear paw, swiped his left palm with his razor-sharp claws, then pressed his bleeding hand against the tear in her scalp. Watching, praying she would live through the change, he caught her fingers in his once again human right hand and pressed her knuckles to his lips. Feeling vulnerable was a new sensation for Daryll. A sensation he hated. "Forgive me, Zoe," he whispered. "Don't go. Stay with me."

# Chapter 22

Within an hour of Daryll's call, Nate had the ranch as prepared as possible in such a short time. Since silver wasn't poisonous to the panthers like it was to the wolves and, to a lesser degree, the bears, Nate stationed the panthers in the large oak and pecan trees surrounding the central compound. The children were gathered in the basement of the main house, with Snarl, Janelle, Cynthia, and Dottie assigned to guard them.

Crane's bears volunteered to hide in the dark in their bear forms. While silver poisoning would kill bears, too, it took more silver, and the bears were more difficult to kill with firearms than their human forms, or even true grizzlies. Wolf, panther, and bear teens were stationed inside the main house, keeping watch through darkened windows. They were the last line of defense, should the Huntsmen get through the rest. All the lights were off. Unless the Huntsmen wore night goggles, the *were* had the advantage.

Once all was ready, Nate and Eli sat in wooden rockers on the porch, booted feet propped on the porch rail, waiting for the Huntsmen to arrive. To the Alphas' eyes, the bright full-moon illuminated the courtyard almost as well as the floodlights would.

Striving to display a nonchalance he didn't feel, Nate sipped on a glass of tea. Rocking in slow motion, he kept his eyes on the stars, knowing Koreth was communicating with the pack and would notify him the instant the hunters arrived. Sprawled in the rocker beside him, Eli rocked a little faster, the Lycos staff across his lap. All Nate felt from his brother was confidence and anger. Confidence they could take care of the problem and anger that they needed to.

*They come.* The tight, silent communication came from a dozen *were* voices. Nate gave a single nod and took another sip of tea. Silent in the night, almost too silent for *were* to hear them, Huntsmen stepped into the clearing. All bore weapons, some rifles, others crossbows, or pistols. Without being told, Nate knew the bullets and quarrels were silver. Nate's gaze swept over them, and he took another sip of tea. Five squads of ten Huntsmen fanned across the compound yard, all aiming their weapons at the two Alphas on the porch. One person in each squad wore military grade night goggles.

A switch inside the house flipped and floodlights attached below the porch roof eaves flared, spearing bright light into the compound yard. Curses rang out as five Huntsmen wearing night goggles tore them off. More floodlights around the compound flashed on, spotlighting the Huntsmen.

Dropping his feet to the porch floor and setting his tea glass on the rail, Nate stood up. Eli's rocking chair creaked as he stood and stepped up beside Nate, the Lycos' staff in his left hand. Nate ignored his brother. "What do you want?"

One of the women facing them gasped. "Major," she said to the man in front of her. "He's the one Xandrie shot. The one they called the One-Royal Lycos. The other one is the other Lycos, the one that killed Xandrie."

"You're sure?" asked the major. "They aren't wolves?"

"Yes, Sir. I'm sure. I didn't see them as wolves, but they're not human."

Without a word, the major pulled the trigger on his crossbow. His Huntsmen followed his action. The sound of dozens of rifle and pistol shots crashed through the ranch. Just before the shots fired, Eli swept the staff forward. A haze of blue light shimmered across in front of Nate and Eli. Bullets and quarrels stopped three feet in front of them and dropped to the ground.

"Your weapons are useless." Nate's soft voice seemed loud in the silence following the gunshots. Eli at his side, he walked down the wide porch steps. "This ranch and all the people living here are under my protection."

Again, the Huntsmen fired. The blue light shimmered again. Bullets and arrows dropped to the ground in front of Nate. Nate

114

took another step. "You have been lied to. The Triumvirate is using you to destroy the only people who can stop them. The only people who can save you."

Nate raised his hands, palms up. Blue light gathered in his palms. Shaking his hands as if ridding himself of water drops, he motioned toward the group. Rifles, pistols, and crossbows wrenched from their hands and flew through the air to smash against a large oak tree. The crash of weapons merged with the gasps of the Huntsmen. "You are helping the destroyers enslave humans."

Pulling knives from their scabbards, the Huntsmen slowly advanced toward Nate. Nate sighed and raised his hands again. Gunshots thundered behind the house. A wolf howled in pain. Roars, howls, yowls, screams, and breaking glass filled the night. Nate heard the back-door crash, and then more shouts, breaking glass, and furniture splintering and crashing. He turned toward the house. At the same moment, the Huntsmen in the courtyard ran forward, trying to overcome Nate and Eli by sheer numbers.

In an instant, Nate shifted into Lycos, his roar resounding. His massive muscled arm swept out, knocking the first wave to the ground. Others swarmed over their fallen friends, jumping at him. Beside him, Eli's Lycos snarled. Nate threw the Huntsmen away from him, uncaring that bones were broken with the force of his toss. Roaring bears charged out of the shadows, knocking silver-bladed knives from the hunter's hands. Some Huntsmen jerked spare pistols from holsters, screaming their rage and terror of being caught between the two Lycos and the bears charging them. Behind the bears, panthers leaped from trees and sped into the fray, snarling, yowling, and swiping massive claws at the attacking humans.

Nate threw another human away from him and left his pack to deal with them. With Eli at his side, he raced for the house. Human screams tore into the night, both inside and behind the house. Nate threw open the front door and flicked on the living room light. Huntsmen had used the distraction from the main group to attack the house from the back. Seven humans, some bleeding from panther, bear, or wolf bites and claws, faced the back wall, hands pressed to the wall above their heads. Others still fought in the backyard against bears and panthers.

The teens in *were* form growled and snarled at the Huntsmen, holding them captive. In the center of the living room, Adrian sat on the floor, legs crossed, Amelie unconscious in his lap. Adrian had a throw from the couch draped over Amelie. He pressed a corner of the throw against her shoulder. Amelie's blood saturated the throw. Adrian's breathing ragged, he looked up at Nate, eyes wide and face pale.

"She's been shot, Alpha. I can't stop the bleeding."

Silver bullets prevented her blood's ability to clot. Without help, she would bleed out. Nate's Lycos roared his anger, then dropped to one knee beside them. "Turn the humans around. Let them see."

Grunts and moans came from the humans against the wall as the teen *were* forced them to turn. One massive clawed hand held above Amelie's shoulder, the Lycos muttered words of power. Blue light shimmered around his hand, then streamed to the girl's shoulder. Her hair fluttered in the flow of energy, brushing against her forehead. Amelie moaned, then sighed and settled into Adrian's arms as if sleeping. The bullet in her shoulder slowly backed out and flew into the Lycos' waiting palm, then her natural wolf healing took over. The wound closed and healed. Lycos stroked her hair away from her eyes, then gently blew on her.

Blue light illuminated the breath that flowed to the girl, then bathed her face. She took a deep breath and opened her eyes. Blinking, she looked up at Lycos and smiled. "Alpha."

Lycos stroked her cheek with the back of his hand, then stood and looked at the Huntsmen. His gaze hardened, and he snarled. He waved a hand. Blue light flickered over the humans, then expanded beyond the walls of the house. All the Huntsmen collapsed, unconscious.

116

Shimmering into Nate, the Alpha split into two, his wolf rushing through the pack, to determine if any others were hurt. There were cuts and scratches, but Amelie was the only one shot. Koreth returned to him and they were one. Nate's Alpha energy flowed through his pack, forcing silver contamination from their wounds.

Gesturing to the unconscious humans, Nate jerked his head at the door. "Bring these and the Huntsmen out back to the compound yard and put them with those out front."

The wolves, bears, and panthers shifted to human. The Huntsmen were lifted and moved to the front yard. Nate exited through the front door and walked down the steps. As soon as all were brought to the front, Nate took a quick count. Seventy Huntsmen.

Nate looked across the yard at the injured and bleeding Huntsmen. With a wave of his hand, the Huntsmen woke. The bears, now in human form, walked through the Huntsmen, forcing those able to kneel to the Alpha. Movement in the trees behind the Huntsmen caught Nate's attention. Twenty *were* animals, wolf, bear, panther, fox, and lion, not pack, walked out of the trees and surrounded the courtyard. Almost immediately, six Jeeps drove around the warehouse and stopped. In the first Jeep, the General stood and nodded to Nate.

"Looks like you didn't need us, after all, Colonel."

Nate crossed his arms and raised an eyebrow. "Why are you here, General?"

The General ignored him. Instead, he studied the men and women on their knees. "We'll take them off your hands, so you won't have to deal with them."

"And do what with them?"

"You don't need to worry about that, Colonel. We'll handle it from here."

Nate shook his head. "No. I won't release them to you."

"Colonel..."

"No, General."

117

"I could just take them, you know."

Nate grinned and jerked his chin toward the shifters the General brought with him. "You think they'll obey you rather than me?"

General Brighton took a step forward. "Nate..."

Nate shifted to his Royal Lycos form. He swept his hand toward the *were*, both those of his pack and those the General brought. "Shift."

Immediately, all *were* shifted to human. Without a word, all the *were* save Eli dropped to their knees, their heads bowed. Nate's Lycos looked at Brighton. "That's how it is, General. I may not have been crowned, as yet, but they accept me as *Were* King. They will obey you only in so far as your commands do not go against me."

The General sighed. "I know. Secretary Bianchi explained all that."

"Then you know you can't take the Huntsmen if I won't release them."

"I could call an airstrike."

"You could." Lycos shimmered into Nate. "If you do, none here will be hurt, but you will cause a human-*were* war no one wants."

"Thought you were supposed to protect the *were*."

"I am. I am also commanded to protect humans. These people will not be taken from me without my approval."

Peyton stepped into the compound clearing. Nate motioned for him to come closer. "Peyton, do you know these people?"

Peyton slung his rifle strap over his shoulder and walked through the humans and *were*, all still on their knees. When he reached Nate's side, he turned, swept his gaze over the crowd, and nodded. "Some of them."

Nate cleared his throat and sent a command through Koreth for the *were* to stand. As the *were* came to their feet, he looked again at Peyton. "Get the tents out of the warehouse. Set them up in the field where the bears lived until their homes were

118

ready. Disarm the Huntsmen and assign tents to them, or have their commanding officers assign tents."

He turned to the Huntsmen. For a moment, he hesitated, then used his Royal Command Voice on them. "This battle is over. Retire to the field. Do not attempt to attack anyone or try to leave. Obey Colonel Marston in all he commands. Until I give further instructions, you are prisoners. Food, water, and medical care will be provided as needed. I will meet with your officers tomorrow morning." He waved his hand toward the field. "Go, now."

Several of the Huntsmen struggled to disobey but couldn't. One of the General's vampire soldiers shoved a woman for moving too slow. Nate growled. Everyone, human, *were*, and vampire froze. "They will not be mistreated!"

The soldier glared at him and motioned at his fellow soldiers. "You may be their king, wolf, but not mine."

Most of the humans gasped when Nate's eyes glowed bright turquoise. "I am your King, too, vampire!" He took a step toward the man. The man opened his mouth to retort, blinking when he couldn't speak. His hand clutched his throat. Nate forced him to shift into a vampire, his teeth elongating and face paling, his eyes glowing a bright, sickly, malevolent whitish yellow.

Nate walked through the crowd of humans, ignoring their efforts to shrink from him. He stopped in front of the vampire and pressed his right palm to the vampire's forehead. A blue light flashed. The vampire screamed and fell unconscious. Nate stepped back and let him fall, then shook his head. He turned and looked at Brighton. "This soldier is a V-Triumph spy."

He raised his palm and aimed the blue light at each of the other four vampires Brighton brought with him, and then at Brighton. The light faded, and Nate dropped his hand to his side. "The rest of the vampires are loyal to you. The Huntsmen stay here. Any of your soldiers who fear retribution is welcome to stay here, too."

Nate tapped his booted toe against the man at his feet. "This one, you can have."

# Chapter 23

Birds chirped in the trees outside the office window as the early morning sun warmed the ranch. Nate stood at the window, watching Jonathan and Peyton supervise while the captured Huntsmen set up tents formerly used by the werebear families. Between the tents and the compound grounds, tables laden with paper plates, napkins, sandwich bread, lunch meats, cheeses, chips, condiments, sodas, coffee, and water were set up for the Huntsmen. He shook his head and muttered, "I think we need more tents."

In the picnic shelter, the pack tended injured Huntsmen. Ten Huntsmen sustained broken bones and other injuries. Nate wasn't sure what to do with them. While he could help *were* to heal, he didn't have the same power when it came to humans. There was no way he could take so many to the hospital without coming to the notice of local police. After Zoe was attacked in the emergency room, he wasn't entirely sure they would survive a visit to the hospital, anyway.

The RV Peyton and Daryll took to Corpus Christi backed into the parking slot set aside for it. Paige, Phillip, and two women Nate didn't know stepped off the RV and started walking toward the house. Movement in the trees caught his attention. Daryll walked hand-in-hand with Zoe. Nate's gaze swept past them, then jerked back to Zoe. Dried blood matted her hair. She and Daryll walked as if they were reluctant to reach the house. Peyton left the campground and walked to Daryll. The two younger Marston's and the women with them joined the group. After a short conversation, they all continued toward the house.

Nate watched them approach for a moment, decided to wait until Peyton and Daryll arrived to start the meeting, then turned to face his Alpha Council, Eli, Renate, and General Brighton. Gathered around the conference table, they waited for him to decide what to do with the Huntsmen. The Huntsmen Major, face devoid of emotion, stood at parade rest at the back wall. Snarl stood to the right and behind Nate, his back to the wall, and his gaze moving constantly to assure Nate's and Janelle's safety.

"Daryll and Peyton are back. We'll start the meeting with their report." Nate leaned forward and rested his elbows on the conference table. A knock sounded at the door, and Daryll stuck his head in. Nate motioned for him to enter. The three Marston's, Zoe, and two women dressed as civilians stood behind him.

Daryll cleared his throat, then swallowed. He glanced over his shoulder at Peyton, then took a deep breath, stood straight, and stepped into the room. Nate tilted his head to the left and noted Daryll's apprehension. "The council is waiting for you."

Daryll swallowed again. "Sir, we have Zoe's mother and her aunt."

Nate glanced at the vacant expression on the face of one woman, then looked at the defiance on the other woman's face. He waved toward the Huntsman major. "Put them over there."

Daryll nodded, clasped them both by the arm, and pulled them to the back wall next to the Huntsman. As Daryll turned to face the Alpha Council, the mate bond between the bear and Zoe snapped into Nate's mind. Anger gushed, blasting Daryll to his knees. Face down, Daryll endured Nate's fury without a word.

"I forbade it!"

"No!" Zoe jumped in front of Daryll. Nate's anger struck her. Zoe moaned and dropped to her knees in front of Daryll. Nate shook his head, trying to dispel the anger that coursed through him when he realized Daryll not only mated Zoe but changed her. When Zoe shouted, then dropped to the floor, Daryll looked up. He caught Zoe as she toppled toward him. Shaking with anger, the werebear surged to his feet, Zoe in his arms. "She was dying, Alpha." Daryll's shout became a whisper. "I couldn't let her die."

Nate closed his eyes and bowed his head, strove to harness

his roiling mind. After a tense minute, he took a deep breath and sighed his anger out. He opened his eyes and looked at Daryll. "Tell me."

"We had an accident on the way to help with the battle. Her head was re-injured." Daryll's eyes gleamed. His Adam's apple bobbed. "I could feel her dying, Nate." He shook his head and whispered, "I couldn't...wouldn't let her die. She's my mate. Even if I die for disobedience. I couldn't do it."

Nate stood very still. Koreth was silent, no help at all. Beside him, Janelle rolled her chair away from the table and stood. She put a gentle hand on his bicep. "Nate."

Only his head moved when he looked down at his mate. *Janelle?*

She gave him a sad smile. *Would you have done any different had I been injured? Even if you were given specific command not to?*

*I would save you at any cost.*

She nodded. *As I would you, Nate.* With a pat on his arm, she sat back down.

Nate took a cleansing breath and looked back at Daryll. He walked around the table and placed his palm over Zoe's eyes. A soft blue light touched her face. When he moved his hand, she opened her eyes. Nate caught her gaze with his, his mind gently entering hers. He found no anger, no fear of the mating bond. Instead, he found acceptance and joy. He smiled at her, then looked at Daryll. "This mating is sanctioned. You have my blessing."

When Zoe squirmed, Daryll set her on her feet, his hands on her shoulders. She smiled at Nate. "Thank you, Alpha."

Nate glanced at the two women they brought in with them. "They are?"

"My mother, Maria, and my Aunt Gisele, sir."

His gaze flicked over Gisele, then lingered on Maria.

"Alpha?"

"Zoe?"

Zoe bit her lip. "My mom was hurt when Daryll pulled

information from her. Can you help her?"

*This is not the time.* Nate frowned at Koreth's growl. He looked again at Maria and sighed. "Take her to Dottie, Zoe. I can't heal humans, but I'll come to see what I can do after the council session." He glanced at Gisele. "Your aunt stays here."

Zoe bowed her head. "Thank you, Sir." She took her mother's hand and led her from the room.

When the door closed behind her, Nate looked at Daryll, then Peyton. "Well, sit down, you're both late." He smothered the grin that tried to show as they both rushed to their council seats. Glancing again at Gisele and the Huntsman Major, he sighed. He nodded at Philip and Paige and motioned for them to stay, then returned to his chair. He swiveled and stared out the window at the clouds until he felt himself in control again, then faced the council.

# Chapter 24

Peyton slid into the chair reserved for him as a member of Nate's Alpha Council. Not that he really belonged there. However, as a changeling wolf who was formerly a Colonel in the Huntsmen, Nate ordered him to sit on the council. Peyton wasn't sure how much help he could be, but it gave him a chance to see just how much of what the Triumvirate taught was... Without cursing, he wasn't even sure what words to use to describe Triumvirate ideology and propaganda used to convince Huntsmen to help the vampires kill off the *were*.

When Nate asked Daryll to report about the trip to Corpus Christi, Peyton took the opportunity to glance at the Huntsman Major. Peyton remembered him. Jim Feller. The expression of anger and betrayal the major threw at him didn't surprise him. *He doesn't know the Triumvirate are vampires. Wonder what he'll think when he does?* Peyton blinked and turned his attention back to Nate.

Nate raised an eyebrow at him. "Have anything to add to the report, Peyton?"

"No, sir. After I left Daryll and Zoe, I came to the main compound. The fighting was already over when I got here."

"You said you know some of the Huntsmen?"

"Yes, Sir." Peyton jerked his chin to indicate the major. "That's Major Jim Feller."

Nate glanced at Feller then looked back at Peyton. The Alpha scratched his neck and sucked air between his teeth. "You're assigned liaison between the Council and the Huntsmen we captured. If we need more tents or other supplies, let Jonathan know, and he'll order them for you." After another glance at the major's hostile expression, Nate rubbed the back of his neck. "Either later today, or early tomorrow, I'll start working with them one-on-one, starting with the Major. Until the geas are removed and they agree not to leave, you will work with Daryll and his Enforcers to keep them in the tent area. Daryll's in charge of the guard rotation."

"Yes, Sir. And the injured?"

Nate turned to the general. "I can't send so many to the emergency room. Do you have field doctors available?"

The general frowned and nodded. "I'll call them in as soon as the meeting is over." Peyton bit his lip and considered the general's expression. For some reason, the man was unhappy.

"Peyton, Daryll said you brought back computers and memory drives. Turn those over to Janelle." When Marston nodded, Nate looked at Janelle, his expression softening. Peyton wondered if Major Feller could see the bond between the Alpha and his mate as easily as the *were* did.

"Janelle, do you need anyone to help you search the computers and memory for records of our misappropriated funds?"

A gasp sent Peyton's gaze to Gisele. Her frantic eyes darted from Janelle to Nate, then to Peyton. Peyton ignored the fear on Gisele's face, glancing back at Nate. Janelle finished the note she was writing into the meeting records and nodded. "I'll ask Reese to work with me. Not sure anyone told you, but the kid is an absolute wizard when it comes to computer devices. Even if records are password protected, he can open them for me. With his help, I should be able to locate our missing funds. Or at least what's left of them."

Beside Peyton, Daryll swallowed. "Sir?"

"Daryll?"

He motioned toward Gisele. "If it's okay, my family will guard Gisele and Zoe's mom."

Nate considered Daryll's suggestion then nodded. His gaze went to Gisele. Peyton turned again to look at the prisoners. Gisele tried to hide her fear, but her face was pale, and she was trembling. Peyton took a breath and squared his shoulders. "Nate?"

Nate quirked an eyebrow at Peyton without speaking.

"I'm not sure I'm much help here. I have some field medic training, as does Gisele. With permission, I could take Gisele to the picnic shelter and help with the injured."

Nate turned back to Gisele. "Will you give us your password?" He tilted his head. "We'll figure it out anyway, but it would save us all some time."

Gisele sucked her bottom lip into her mouth but didn't answer.

The Alpha nodded. "Take her to the shelter, Peyton. Give whatever help you can. Take two of the Enforcers with you. I don't want the prisoners attacking you."

# Chapter 25

After Peyton took Gisele out of the office, Nate sighed, then looked at General Brighton's angry expression. *He still wants us to give him the Huntsmen we captured.* Nate considered Koreth's assessment. Whether the prisoners went to the general depended on what he wanted with them. "Okay, General, tell me why you think the Huntsmen should be turned over to you."

General Brighton pursed his lips, face wrinkling like he had a bad taste in his mouth. "We have facilities for captured Huntsmen. You don't."

"What do you intend to do with them if I give them to you?"

"That's classified."

Nate studied the General and shrugged. "Then they stay here."

"Colonel..."

"General!" Nate stood up, palms flat against the table, and leaned toward his former commanding officer. A fleeting glimmer of fear entered the general's eyes. Nate's gaze speared him with a warning. "I already told you their safety is my charge. If you can't tell me what you're planning to do with them, I won't release them."

General Brighton crossed his arms over his chest. "So, you're going to what? Set them up as refugees in a tent city?"

"I'm going to release them." Nate's quiet statement seemed to catch the general off guard.

"You what?"

"I'll remove their rings and release them."

For the first time, the Huntsman Major's eyes met Nate's gaze. The Major blinked and swallowed. Other than that, Nate saw no reaction. He turned his gaze back to Brighton.

No longer belligerent, the General frowned and rested his forearms on the conference table. "Removing their rings will kill them."

"No, General. We've learned how to remove their rings without killing them." Nate straightened his back and rolled his shoulders. *Being King sucks!* Koreth's bark of laughter echoed in the back of his mind. Nate shook his head to clear his thoughts. "I'll remove the kill geas the vampires put in their minds. After that, we'll try to explain to them what has happened, what the V-Triumph are, and what their goals are. The Huntsmen who have previously been exposed to truth have abandoned the Triumvirate teachings."

Brighton swept his gaze around the room at the Alpha Council, then looked back at Nate. "They won't all abandon what they've been taught. What about them?"

"I won't kill them, and I won't allow you to bury them in some federal prison. General, I'm not the enemy. You know that. Why are you pushing this?"

General Brighton blinked, then shook his head. "I know you're not the enemy, Nate." He glanced at Nate's father, Major Rollins, then looked back at Nate. The Alpha felt the difference in Brighton's attitude when he finally decided to trust the *were*. "It's need to know..." He raised his palm toward Nate when Nate started to speak. "But...you have top clearance. Your council..." He shook his head. "If you trust your council, I will trust them."

"If I didn't trust them, General, they wouldn't be part of my council."

The general scratched his jaw. "Captured Huntsmen are..." He looked up at Nate. "Those amenable to the truth become part of the Elite after the geas is removed and retraining."

Nate closed his mouth. The humans in the Elite were former Huntsmen? He waited for the general to continue.

"It's how we grow our numbers without exposing *were* to other humans."

Nate glanced at his dad. "Did you know this?"

Rollins shook his head. "I didn't know what the Elite was until after I found out you are *were*. All I knew was that certain applications were selected for special training."

"Only those in the unit know, Nate. And not all of them." General Brighton glanced at Eli, then back to Nate. "Those who don't know are like you and Eli. Highly trained in martial arts and self-defense before you even get to us. Surely, you remember how difficult it was to join the Elite."

Nate and Eli exchanged glances, and Nate nodded at the general. "I remember. So, the Elite is made up of highly trained humans, such as you believed me and Eli to be, *were*, vampires, and former Huntsmen?"

"That's about it."

Nate leaned back in his chair. "How many refuse to retrain? What happens to them?"

The general squirmed in his chair and avoided Nate's gaze. "Fifteen to twenty percent refuse to accept. They are..." The anger and sadness the general felt were like a grey fog around him. "The Triumvirate destroyed them, took their... I suppose some would say they took their souls. They no longer are able to live without the geas."

"What happens to them?"

"I don't know. We turn them over to others." The general's statement rang true.

Nate steepled his hands and leaned his chin on his thumbs. He studied Brighton and frowned at the general's annoyed expression. Nate's charge forced him to shoulder responsibility for the humans' well-being. "I won't give them to you if I don't know what happens to them, General. I can't. For all I know, they'll end up in a shallow grave somewhere or some underground prison."

Nate sighed and pinched the bridge of his nose with his thumbs. He was exhausted after the battle last night and so tired of sighing. Sooner or later, he needed some sleep. "Find out. If you want them, find out. Otherwise, I'll figure out how to deal with them."

Lips pressed tight, the general nodded. "I'll see what I can learn. In the meantime?"

"We'll do what we can here. Any who wish to join the Elite after the geas is removed are welcome to do so. Call in your field medics and provide the care the injured need."

# Chapter 26

Nate dismissed all but Janelle, Eli, Renate, General Brighton, Snarl, and the Huntsman major. The major's gaze followed those who left until the door shut behind them, then turned to look at Nate. As scents associated with his council decreased, the acrid stench of fear grew, but the major kept his head up, gaze on Nate.

For the first time since he was brought to the room, the major spoke. "You're not human, but you're not a werewolf, either. What are you?"

"I'm not human." Nate watched the man's courage falter. "I am a wolf and more than a wolf. I am Lycos." He gestured toward Eli. "As is my brother."

The human frowned. "Never heard of Lycos."

Nate leaned forward, elbows on the table, left hand folded in the right, his chin resting on his clasped fist. He shrugged. "Not really important, right now. Why did you come here?"

The major's eyes flicked from face to face, then settled back on Nate. "You captured one of our commanders."

"Marston? Maybe. In my mind, I was saving him from you and your kind."

"Saving him?"

"He was left alone with us. He seemed to think he would die for it, so I brought him with me when I came home." Nate tilted his head and his eyes narrowed. "I suppose that means you will die, too, since you are alone with us."

Major Feller swallowed but kept his mouth shut.

"What do you know of the Triumvirate?"

Feller blinked, then sneered. "You think I'd tell you?"

"You will. Whether you want to or not. I just thought I would give you the option to cooperate. Otherwise, you might end up as damaged as Zoe's mother is."

"What did you do to her?"

Nate sucked air through his teeth. "Feller, the Triumvirate have been killing humans since long before the Huntsmen were organized. Our task is to stop them."

Feller laughed and shook his head. "And I'm supposed to take the word of a wolf? I don't think so."

"Does the Triumvirate know I'm the Royal King?"

"The what?" Feller's wide-eyed gaze turned to each of the others in the room, then he looked back at Nate. Nate smelled confusion, not lies.

"I am the Royal King of prophecy. It is my task to destroy the V-Triumph."

"Never heard of them."

"The V-Triumph control the Triumvirate."

The Major laughed. "And they are? What? Monsters, like you?"

"Worse than me, Major Feller. They are vampires using you and other Huntsmen to destroy the only hope humans have."

"Vampires are a myth."

Nate raised both eyebrows. Feller believed what he just said. Nate looked at the general. "Will you show him?"

Annoyance plain on his face, the general stood and walked around the table, stopping an arm's length from the major. "Look at me."

Feller gazed at Brighton. As Brighton's fangs distended and his eyes brightened then became a burning, sickly, whitish yellow, Feller gasped. "What are you?"

"I am a vampire. The only difference between me and those you serve is I don't feel the need to consume human blood." Brighton's pale fingers fluttered lightly against Feller's neck. "You have fed them, but they took the memory from you."

"I what?"

"I feel the essence of them on you." Brighton looked at Nate. "I can cleanse his memory if you wish."

When Nate nodded, Brighton clamped his hand on the

133

major's shoulder. Nate heard the mental command that froze the major where he stood, his gaze trapped by the general's glowing eyes. Wanting to ensure cleansing was all the general did, Nate sent Koreth into the major's mind following the general. Brighton slipped easily through Feller's thoughts, taking him to the last time he fed the vampires of the Triumvirate. Nate felt as well as heard the major's gasp when his memory of the event was recovered.

Brighton located the geas controlling the major, grasped it and tore it apart. Carefully, he removed his consciousness from the major's mind, squeezed the human's shoulder, then returned to his seat. Nate followed his mind out, saddened by the terror in the major's mind. The major blinked, then blinked again. He looked at Nate. Feller's right hand stroked the left side of his neck as if he could feel where they fed on him. "They're really vampires." It wasn't a question.

Nate nodded. "They are. They've been controlling you and the other Huntsmen for centuries, sending you to kill *were* and feeding on you. To them, you are slaves and food. Nothing more." The man's face paled even more, and he swayed on his feet. Nate waved to an empty chair. "I think you should sit down."

Feller swallowed, then moved to the chair. He sat and bowed his head for several seconds before looking up at Nate. "What do you want from me?"

# Chapter 27

Zoe wrapped a bath sheet around herself and stepped out of the ensuite bathroom in Daryll's room. She walked to the dresser and looked at herself in the mirror. A bear. She was a werebear. Staring into her own eyes in the mirror, her eyebrows furrowed. *I don't look any different.* Her bear snuffled in her mind. *But you feel different.*

Sighing, she acknowledged her bear's thought with a short nod, then picked up the hairbrush on the dresser. After running the brush through her wet hair, she stopped and looked closer at her reflection. "My hair is thicker."

Her bear rumbled an agreement.

A tap on the door was followed by the door opening enough to let Daryll stick his head in the room. "Okay if I come in?"

"Give me a minute to get dressed."

Without a word, he left and shut the door. Zoe dropped the terrycloth sheet and quickly dressed. She folded the sheet and draped it over a chair. "You can come in now."

Daryll came in and sat on the side of the bed, watching as she continued to brush her hair. "Bess put some hair stuff in the top drawer."

Zoe opened the indicated drawer and pulled out a green hair elastic that matched the shirt she wore. Glancing at Daryll in the mirror, she finished pulling her hair into a ponytail, then turned to look at him.

"You look much better, now that you've washed all the blood out of your hair." Daryll twisted his large right hand in the bedspread. "I'm sorry, Zoe. I would never have taken the right to choose from you, if..."

"If I weren't dying?" She tilted her head and studied the misery in his eyes. "I would have died. You know that, right?"

"It's my fault..."

"That I insisted on going with you? That we needed to get to the ranch fast?"

"That I wasn't watching where I was going." His gaze dropped, and he bowed his head.

Zoe took a deep breath and let it out. "So, am I still your mate?"

"What?" Daryll's gaze snapped up to her face.

"Well, you told me I was your mate. Bess and Stella seem to think so, too. Is that still true?"

"Always." His lips pressed tight. "If you can...forgive me."

"For saving my life?"

"For endangering your life."

*Our mate is afraid we will leave him.* Zoe moved to sit beside him. When Daryll's posture stiffened, she picked up his right hand and gently pulled the bedspread from his fingers. "I decided to stay with you before the accident, Daryll."

He looked at her and blinked. "You understand? If you do..."

She nodded and smiled. "I'm your mate, remember?" Grinning, she pushed a wisp of hair off his forehead. "I'm not going anywhere. Besides, you need to help me with my bear." Zoe leaned toward him. "She says her name is Merka."

Daryll's grin bled into his eyes. "Well met, Merka. Darcel greets you."

Zoe laughed at Merka's preening. "I think she likes Darcel."

"She would. They are mates, too." Daryll raised her hand and kissed her knuckles. "As much as I would love to spend more time alone with you, Nate needs help with the Huntsmen."

"Okay." Zoe pulled his hand to her lips and kissed his fingers. "We have our future ahead of us." Pulling her hand from his, she walked back to the dresser and picked up the throwing knives she had removed from her pockets before her shower. After a moment, she put them down, then opened the drawer and pulled out the dagger she wore when she first came to the ranch. She hid it in her clothes and raised an eyebrow at Daryll's expression.

"What?"

"I don't think you need that, now."

She nodded. "I'm sure you're right, but I've known the Huntsmen my entire life. I'll be more comfortable with it than without."

"As you wish." He stood and offered his hand.

Taking it, she walked with him through the house. When they stepped out on the porch, she took a deep breath, memorizing the smells, imprinting on her home. A smile touched her lips. With a light heart, she walked with Daryll to his SUV.

\*\*\*\*\*

The scene at the ranch was controlled chaos. *Were* in human form patrolled the yard between the captured Huntsmen and the house, where the children were still hidden. They no longer stayed in the saferoom in the basement, but instead played in the backroom playroom where the preschool and nursery were set up.

After nursing Ophelia, Janelle gave her into Cynthia's care. Snarl stayed with Cynthia and Ophelia. As long as there were strangers and enemies on the ranch, he would be the baby's personal guard. Janelle went to check on Nate and help feed and process the Huntsmen.

Each of the Huntsmen was brought to a canvas canopy where Nate or Brighton removed the vampire geas from their minds, and their rings were removed. Most of them were stunned to learn their leaders were vampires. A few refused to believe, instead insisting Nate and Brighton were putting lies into their minds. After two nights without sleep, exhaustion settled in Nate's face and Janelle frowned when he staggered.

Catching his arm in her hand, she pulled him toward an empty chair. "Sit down, Nate."

"I can't. There's still too much to do."

137

She huffed at him. "Sit!"

Blinking at her, he sat in the chair she pushed him toward. "Janelle..."

"Nope. Not happening. It's my job to keep you healthy. You need to rest, and you need food." When he opened his mouth to argue, Janelle gave him a fierce frown. "No arguing. Sit there. At least until you get something to eat."

Holding her palm toward him to show she was serious, she glanced around until she located Stella, Daryll's youngest sister, bringing a tray of lemonade to the canopy. "Stella, would you get Nate a couple of sandwiches. I don't think he's eaten since sometime yesterday."

Stella grinned at Nate. "I'll go as soon as I hand out the lemonade."

Nate sighed and accepted the lemonade Stella offered him. Janelle smiled at the girl. "Thank you." With a nod, Stella turned back to her task. Janelle pulled another chair close to Nate and sat with him. "How much is left for you to do?"

Nate wiped his face with his right hand, then rolled his shoulders. "We have about a dozen left to go."

"And then?"

He tried to stop a yawn. Janelle snickered when he yawned anyway, then blinked. "Brighton told me those who refuse to believe will have their memories stripped permanently and be released somewhere on the West Coast. The others will be offered the opportunity to join the Elite."

"You're okay with that?"

Nate reached for her hand and squeezed her fingers. "I don't have a way to care for them here. The general promised me they'll all be safe." His eyes drooped. With a sigh, he leaned back in the chair and closed his eyes.

After a moment, his breathing changed. Janelle grinned at her dozing mate and gently removed her hand from his. Setting his hand on his thigh, she stood and walked to the general. Two soldiers took the man he had just released from the vampire's geas back toward the tent camp in the field beyond the gate.

"You need something to eat, too, General?"

When General Brighton grinned at her, Janelle forced herself not to react to his sharp teeth. "No, thank you. I ate yesterday, so I am good for a few days, yet."

"Just let me know if you need anything."

"I'll do that, Mrs. Rollins."

Janelle pushed some warmth into her smile. She was sure the general wasn't fooled, but she didn't want to be discourteous to a guest. She turned and waved at Zoe and Daryll. Stella walked toward the house, ignoring Daryll's greeting.

He shook his head, annoyance on his face, and he and Zoe walked hand-in-hand toward the canopy. When Zoe stopped to chat with one of the teens, Daryll tugged his hand from hers and continued to the canopy. "Janelle..."

A scream behind Daryll pulled Janelle's gaze beyond him. The man the general just finished with stabbed one of his guards, then attacked the other. After a brief scuffle, he shoved the second guard to the ground and jumped toward Stella.

The teen screamed again and tripped trying to get away from him. Zoe moved so fast, Janelle wasn't sure where she came from. Her hand clasped Stella's arm and jerked the girl to the side. Zoe shoved herself between the oncoming Huntsman and her mate's sister. The girl sprawled on the ground then rolled to her feet and ran toward Daryll.

Janelle blinked at the speed of Zoe's hand as the werebear pulled a dagger from her shirt and met the Huntsman. The man jabbed at Zoe. Slipping to the side, she used his momentum to catch his arm. Twisting, she yanked him off balance, then slammed her elbow into his face. Bone cracked as his nose broke. Blood splattered.

The Huntsman's foot slid in the dew-wet grass. Staggering, he swept his blade past Zoe, slicing the large muscle her of left bicep. Zoe growled. Left arm clamped against her side, she blocked his next strike with her right forearm. She rolled her arm

139

to shove his blade aside. Leaning in, she whirled, brought her blade up beneath his ribs. She stabbed him. Twisting her wrist, she sliced a long, shallow cut across his abdomen. Gasping, the Huntsman staggered back.

Before he could regain control, Daryll caught him from behind and forced him to drop his weapon. Nate pulled Janelle away from the fight area, then stepped around Zoe. His large hand clamped the back of the Huntsman's head. Blue light bathed the crown of the man's head. He gasped and sagged to the ground, unconscious.

Janelle spun to Zoe. Bent at the waist, the pommel of her dagger resting on her knee, the young woman strove to catch her breath. She stared at the Huntsman on the ground, ignoring the blood on her arm. Blood! Janelle forced herself not to gag. "Zoe, you're injured!"

Zoe blinked, looked at Janelle, then glanced at her arm. Her face paled at the sight. "Oh."

Daryll caught her as her legs gave out. He dropped to his knees, leaned her against his chest. "You'll be okay, Zoe. It's not that bad." He pulled a clean, folded bandana from his pocket and wiped away the blood. Even as Janelle watched, the wound began to heal.

Stella shoved past Janelle toward Daryll and Zoe and stumbled. Nate caught her, held her to her feet. "Are you okay, Stella?"

Stella shivered, never taking her gaze from Zoe. A touch of surprise and awe entered her face as she blinked at her brother's mate. "She saved my life."

# Chapter 28

The next morning, with Nate's approval, the general took charge of the Huntsmen. With tents taken down and put away, guards loaded the Huntsmen into three convoy trucks, two for those heading for training, and a third for those who refused to join the Elite. Nate stood on the porch, coffee in his hand, watching while soldiers loaded the former combatants. An hour later, the general's jeep led the trucks down the ranch drive toward the county road.

Nate released the tension that coiled his shoulders. They'd been tight since Daryll called two days ago. His pack was safe again. When the trucks were no longer in sight, the children were allowed to run outside to play in the sun. Nate watched their happy romps and grinned. The Huntsmen would likely come again, but the pack would be ready.

Daryll's SUV pulled up in front of the house. Zoe got out and opened the back door, motioning the two women in the back to get out. Nate pursed his lips. *Janelle, Zoe asked for her mom and aunt to stay on the ranch.*

From inside the house, Janelle silently answered. *Zoe belongs with us, now. Her family, too.*

Nate peered at the clouds drifting by. It seemed more people moved to the ranch every day. His attention moved to the four walking to the house. "Morning."

"Good morning." Daryll motioned toward Zoe's family. "You wanted to meet with us?"

"I did." Nate opened the screen door. "Let's go to the office for a bit." He led them inside and up the stairs. Motioning them to sit around the conference table, he walked to his chair and sat down. For a moment, lips pursed, he studied the two women. "I understand you want to stay here."

After Nate and Dottie treated Maria, her mind was sharp

again. Nate knew Maria struggled with her daughter being a bear shifter but love for her only living child seemed to be her motivation for staying on the ranch. Maria swallowed and nodded. "I'm still not sure I believe all I've been told, but if Zoe is staying here, I want to be here with her."

"To protect her from us."

Maria started to deny it but then nodded. "If necessary."

Nate ignored Zoe's exasperated breath. "Zoe is part of my pack, now. It's my job to ensure she is safe and healthy. She isn't in danger."

Zoe's mom bit her lip. "That's what she said."

"But you don't believe it?"

"I'm...trying."

Nate tilted his head and glanced at Gisele. "And you?"

"You treated Maria, helped her heal from her injury. I saw Zoe heal from the knife wound. Your restraint in dealing with the Huntsman she fought with was, well, I was impressed. I have changed my mind about you and your pack." Gisele raised her left shoulder and dropped it. "I accept that you are a protector, rather than the enemy."

Nate studied the two women for a moment longer, then nodded. "I want you to sell the house you bought with pack funds, Gisele. The proceeds will go into pack accounts. All the money in your personal accounts will be forfeit, as well. But, as Zoe's family, you are welcome to stay here. Your needs will be provided for."

When Gisele didn't complain, Nate continued, "Until I am absolutely convinced you are trustworthy, you will have someone with you at all times. If Zoe or Daryll can't be with you, Peyton Marston will be assigned."

"Fair enough. It's more freedom than you would have in the Huntsman camp. And the funds came from your accounts, anyway." Gisele glanced at Maria, then leaned forward. "Mr. Rollins..."

"Nate."

"Okay, Nate. When the Huntsmen don't return..."

"More will come, eventually. We'll be ready for them." Nate leaned back in his chair, his hands steepled over his chest. "Did the Triumvirate send them, or one of the commanders?"

Gisele shook her head. "HQ commanders decided on this raid. The Triumvirate seldom deals with day-to-day operations of the Huntsmen, but they may step in, now, since they've lost so many in this raid."

"Are the Triumvirate aware of the ranch?"

"Of course. They sent me to the area to keep you under surveillance."

"Surveillance?"

"Mostly through your financials, but there is a camera on the property across from your gate that let me watch to see who came to the ranch and how often."

When Nate's gaze flicked to Daryll, the Enforcer nodded. "I'll find it and remove it, Alpha."

With a nod, Nate turned to Zoe. "When Stella was threatened, you protected her."

Zoe's face reddened. "Stella is my mate's sister. I couldn't let anything happen to her."

"In so doing, you have gained my trust. I understand you are highly trained. Even more so than many of the others. True?"

"Yes, Sir." Zoe squirmed in her seat. "I was training to be a Commander, someday."

Nate sucked air through his teeth. "You know Snarl is Ophelia's personal guard." When Zoe and Daryll nodded, Nate leaned forward. "I need someone who knows how to fight the Huntsmen to be Janelle's guard. Interested?"

Zoe blinked, then looked at Daryll. Daryll spread his hands and shrugged. "It's not my decision, Zoe. I don't own you."

Zoe sat up straighter and smiled. "I would be honored to be Janelle's personal guard, Alpha."

# Chapter 29

Since Eli and Renate were scheduled to leave the next morning, Nate called a meeting of the Alpha Council soon after lunch. When everyone was in their seats and the door closed, he tapped the table twice to indicate the meeting was starting. He nodded at Janelle. In a firm, soft voice, Janelle read the minutes from the previous meeting.

When she finished, Nate looked around. "Anything to add?" No one made suggestions. "Okay, I called you together to discuss our next step. Now that the Huntsmen have been taken care of for the moment, I want to start gathering the Alphas for a meeting."

Nate watched his council members look around the room at each other. "Snarl thinks the Triumvirate won't attack until the actual Council Convention. So..." He leaned forward and smiled. "I want to call each group separately, then after each group accepts me as their king, we will have the Council Convention. At that point, we should be strong enough to overcome the attack, or maybe even take the attack to them."

Eli crossed his arms over his chest and tilted his head to the left. "Who do you want to call first?"

"I think I'll call the cats, first. Panthers, lions, cougars, tigers." Nate looked at Daryll. "Are there others?"

"There are leopards and cheetahs, too," the Enforcer told him.

"Okay. Them, too. I want to call them all at once if we have room for them."

Snarl cleared his throat. "There are about forty clowders and prides worldwide. They will send their Alphas and at least one or two more. Most will leave their betas behind to care for the rest while they're here. At most, you should have a hundred and fifty show up."

Nate tapped his thumb on the table. "Will they have the means to get here?"

Snarl thought for a moment, then shrugged. "If you mean money, some will, some won't."

Nate considered his answer and nodded. "We will cover the expenses for travel if they need it." He glanced at Janelle. "You bought the Bay Inn?"

Janelle looked up from her laptop keyboard. "Yes."

"We'll try to get all the Alpha meetings over in the next two months. Reserve the entire hotel for eight weeks starting the first of next month."

"And if we already have other reservations?"

"Offer to pay for their stay at another area hotel. I don't want a lot of *were* mixing with more humans than necessary."

Eli cleared his throat. "What about the humans working at the inn?"

Nate growled and put his face in his hands. After a moment, he looked up at Eli. "You think they would accept a two-month, paid vacation?"

"Probably, but between us, we don't have enough pack members to staff the inn for two months and keep our pack grounds protected and safe." Eli looked at the ceiling for a moment, then grinned. "Guess we could just lay down the rules of conduct before they arrive and let them know they will be held responsible for any human being hurt."

Nate sighed. "I guess that's the best we can do." He looked at Snarl. "How do I go about calling them here?"

The older man snickered. "The Lycos knows what to do."

Janelle's hand reached out and covered Nate's, stilling his drumming thumb. He glanced at her and winked at her. "Sorry." When she grinned, he smiled and looked back at the others.

"We have two weeks to get ready for the first group to arrive. Janelle, make sure we have the food stores we need. Jonathan, will the SUV's suffice for transportation, or should we consider purchasing or leasing buses?"

Jonathan considered for a moment, then nodded. "Purchasing or leasing buses would probably be better. By the time we could get everyone here using the SUVs, it would be time to take them back to the hotel." He leaned forward. "Unless you want to use the hotel conference rooms for your meetings."

Nate hesitated, not sure that was a good idea. "Let's think that through before deciding."

Jonathan nodded.

Nate turned to Eli. "You're going home tomorrow morning, right?"

Eli smiled at Renate, then grinned at Nate. "Yep. We've already been gone longer than we should have been."

"About what I expected." Nate looked at Daryll. "I need you to beef up security. Cut the building teams in half and put half on security."

"Yes, sir. I'll get to it."

Nate turned to Jonathan and Ben. "After this last attack, I want everyone…" he turned and looked at his mate, "…including you, Janelle. I want everyone to start training. Order enough guns and ammunition that everyone who qualifies can be armed. Everyone, all the girls too, five years and up will have self-defense classes, starting Monday."

He shook his head at the surprise on Jonathan's face. "I know Randal didn't think women should be fighters, but if Zoe hadn't been there, Stella might have died just because she couldn't protect herself. It might also have helped when the former clowder Queen attacked the ranch."

Zoe cleared her throat and waved her hand. "What about knife fighting, Nate? Shouldn't that be included since most of the Huntsmen carry knives?"

When Koreth growled his approval, Nate looked at Zoe, then nodded. "That's a good idea. Think you could teach the women and girls?"

"I can."

"Then you're in charge of teaching the ladies, while Peyton

can teach the guys." He glanced at Peyton with an eyebrow raised.

Peyton bowed his head briefly, then looked up. "I'll be happy to, Nate."

Nate looked at each member of the council. "Anything else?"

When no one mentioned anything else, Nate stood up. Throwing his head back, he shimmered into Lycos, then smirked at Janelle when he realized he had prevented ripping his jeans without thinking about it. Her eyes crinkled at him, but she didn't mention it aloud.

Lycos' steps thundered to the window and he looked across the ranch acreage. The evening was just beginning to settle in, the sun below the horizon. Lifting his head, he closed his eyes, thought about the Alphas he wanted to contact, and sent a narrowly focused thought across the world, assured each would hear the thought in his own language.

*Werecats, come to meet your King!* Lycos followed the roaring thought with contact details as it sped to the Alphas of each pack, clowder, murder, and pride of all the werecats. *Come! Your King so commands!*

**The next book in the series *is Wolf's Reign.***

# Thank You!

Thank you for reading, *Wolf's Trust*, the fifth book in the Texas Ranch Wolf Pack series.

# Please Leave a Review

Reviews are the lifeblood of books in today's market. If you read this book, please take the time to leave an honest review.

Reviews are not book reports. They are just a few words to let other readers know how you liked or didn't like the book.

Authors, especially indie authors, depend on reviews to help readers find their books. Good or bad reviews help an author on the journey as an author.

You can also find Lynn Nodima's books and stories at: www.lynnnodima.com.

# Lynn's Books

**The Texas Ranch Wolf Pack Series**
Wolf's Man
Wolf's Claim
Wolf's Mission
Wolf's Huntsman
Wolf's Trust
Wolf's Reign
Wolf's Queen
Wolf's Enemy
Wolf's Rage
Wolf's Quest
Wolf's Guard
Wolf's Duty

**Texas Ranch Wolf Pack World**
Wolf's Sorrow
Wolf's Mate
Wolf's Heart
Wolf's Dragon
Wolf's Princess
Wolf's Son

**Texas Ranch Wolf Pack Box Sets**
Wolf's Destiny: Books 1-6
Wolf's Victory: Books 7-12

# *More Fiction by Lynn Nodima*

## The Tala Ridge Shifters Series
Tala Ridge Alpha
Tala Ridge Storm

## Short Story Collections
Dreams in the Night

## Short Stories
Alas, Atlantis!
All I Done
Design Defect
Heart Failure
A Relative Truth
Trinity's Sorrow
The Viper Pit

## The Billionaire Brothers
Holiday Rescue
Not for Sale
Jax's Story (TBD)

**Visit** www.lynnnodima.com **to learn more!**
**Email Lynn at** lynn@lynnnodima.com!

Follow Lynn Nodima on Amazon.com to receive a notification when new books are published!

Made in the USA
Las Vegas, NV
15 February 2024